His Untamed Desire

Moon Shifter Series

Katie Reus

Praise for the Novels of Katie Reus

"All the elements I like . . . a fun, emotional, sexy, suspenseful series."
—*Paranormal Haven*

"An extremely sensual tale filled with exotic characters."
—*Night Owl Reviews*

"A vivid world filled with sexy shifters, explosive danger, and enough sexual tension to set the pages on fire. A fabulous paranormal romance!"
—**Alexandra Ivy, *New York Times* bestselling author**

"A sexy, well-crafted paranormal romance that succeeds with smart characters and creative world building."
—*Kirkus Reviews*

"This series keeps getting better and better."
—*Joyfully Reviewed*

"Reus has definitely hit a home run with this series... This book has mystery, suspense, and a heart-pounding romance that will leave you wanting more."
—*Nocturne Romance Reads*

"If you like your romance hot with plenty of buildup and a plot that sucks you right in, *Primal Possession* is simply a must read."
—*A Book Obsession*

"You'll look forward to visiting this world again soon!"
—*RT Book Reviews*

"Reus crafts a fast-paced action story... *Alpha Instinct* is awesome: an engrossing page-turner that I enjoyed in one sitting. Reus offers all the ingredients I love in a paranormal romance."
—*Book Lovers Inc.*

"Prepare yourself for the start of a great new series! . . . I'm excited about reading more about this great group of characters."
—*Fresh Fiction*

"A well-plotted, excellently delivered emotional and sensual ride that grabs hold and doesn't let go! . . . Ms. Reus delivers mystery, suspense, and a romance nothing short of heart pounding!"
  —*Night Owl Reviews*

"A strong book full of mystery, intrigue, and a new world to explore. . . . I thoroughly enjoyed this one as I suspect lovers of the paranormal romance genres will do as well!"
  —*Ramblings from a Chaotic Mind*

"If you're looking for a new shifter romance to sink your teeth in, then look no further. *Alpha Instinct* is action-packed with a solid romance that will keep the reader on the edge of [her] toes! . . . Highly recommended for fans of Rachel Vincent's Werecat series."
  —*Nocturne Romance Reads*

"Sexy alphas, kick-ass heroines, and twisted villains will keep you turning the pages...a winner."
  —**Caridad Piñeiro, *New York Times* bestselling author**

"Sexy military romantic suspense!"
  —*USA Today*

"Both romantic and suspenseful, a fast-paced sexy book full of high stakes action."
  —*Heroes and Heartbreakers*

"Reus's passionate and protective alpha-warrior shifters come alive on the page as she continues to deftly expand her intricate paranormal world integrating beings born of myth and imagination... Readers can expect a fast-paced action-packed read including battle scenes and nail-biting suspense."
—*Happy Ever After, USA Today Blog*

"...a wild hot ride for readers. The story grabs you and doesn't let go." —*New York Times* **bestselling author, Cynthia Eden**

"Future books in this series are definitely on my auto buy list and I'm looking forward to getting to know the rest of the O'Connor family." —*Feeling Fictional*

"...the characters are heartwarming and energetic; the romance is provocative and seductive." —*The Reading Cafe*

About the Book

She's ready to make her move...

Lupine shifter Daphne's recent move back home gives her a chance with the fierce and sexy male she's always wanted: jaguar shifter Hector. She plans to show him she's all grown up, and more than enough woman for him. But a vampire from her past has been harassing her and will stop at nothing to make her his.

He's not letting her go this time...

Hector knows Daphne can take care of herself, but he immediately steps in to protect her from a stalker. He's wanted the sweet and sensual she-wolf for years and won't let anything come between them now. With circumstances forcing them to share a roof, Hector won't hide his attraction toward her any longer. But Daphne underestimates her stalker's persistence and it might be too late for Hector to keep the woman he loves safe.

Chapter 1

Daphne ignored the appreciative looks and whistles she received as she strode down Chartres Street. She still had a few more blocks to go until she reached the Full Moon Bar, right in the heart of the French Quarter. It was owned by Angus, her Alpha, and she hadn't been there in years. She'd been back home in New Orleans for a month, but hadn't had a chance to get out yet since she was still getting settled into her new program at school.

Tonight, she planned to let loose. Part of her hoped that Hector, the sexiest shifter she'd ever laid eyes on, was working tonight and saw her looking like she did. She'd changed a lot while away at Duke, grown more comfortable in her skin, and after the way he'd rejected her four years ago, she wanted him to drool over her. Petty? Yeah, probably. She just didn't care. If she hadn't been best friends with his sister, Leta, it would have been easier to ignore him back then. After crushing on him throughout high school, it was beyond time for her to move on.

At five foot nine Daphne was tall for a female, and she'd worn three-inch heeled boots to give herself even more height. Her boots laced up to her thighs and the black minidress she had on was skintight. Not her normal style, but she was going to make sure she had Hector's attention.

Let's see him ignore me now.

In order to avoid a very intoxicated couple yelling at each other on the sidewalk, she stepped down onto the cobblestone street and veered around them. The back of her neck prickled in awareness as she stepped back onto the sidewalk. Glancing around, she self-consciously tugged her cropped leather jacket together. As a lupine shifter there wasn't much out there that she couldn't defend herself against, but lately she'd felt as if someone or something was *watching* her. She didn't have any proof, but she never ignored her innate animal ability to sense danger. It had never failed her.

Picking up her pace, Daphne hurried around the corner. Her shoulders relaxed a bit as she neared the Full Moon Bar. It was in full swing tonight. Music from a live band streamed out as a group of about ten shifters entered. A few seconds later, she did the same. Spicy food, alcohol, the press of different bodies—the scents accosted her at once. Since the majority of people who frequented it had oversensitive hearing, they normally kept the volume down. But with the live band, everything was rowdier tonight. She didn't mind. Not since she was here to have a good time.

One of the security guys started to ask her for her ID but then blinked as he recognized her. Even though she'd been back a month she'd only seen her Alpha, her parents, and a few friends. She grinned at Saul, one of her packmates. He was only about a decade older than her. Big and broad-shouldered, just like most of the members of her pack, he had dirty-blond hair and near-black eyes. He stared at her, his mouth gaping for a long moment.

"Put your tongue back in," she finally muttered. She didn't look *that* different than before. She was really glad that even though they were part of the same pack, they weren't even remotely related. It would have made the way he was checking her out gross.

"You look fucking hot!"

Her face flamed at his words, but she rolled her eyes. "Is this how you talk to the ladies? No wonder you're still single."

He just smiled and pulled her into a giant bear hug. Even with her added height, he pulled her off the ground. Laughing, she wrapped her arms around his neck. As she hugged him, she spotted Hector out of the corner of her eye, but it was clear he wasn't working. He was sitting at a high-top table... with a very pretty woman.

Daphne's canines and claws ached, ready to unsheathe and draw blood. *Jeez.* What was wrong with her? Refusing to fully look in Hector's direction, she kept her focus on Saul as he put her down. "How've you been?"

He shrugged, eyeing her with frank, male interest. "Better now that you're here."

She let out a sigh. "Seriously? That's all you have to say to me?"

He grinned in that boyish way that she knew had charmed the panties off a lot of ladies. "I'm just messing with you, though you do look good. I was glad to hear you were back from college. Why aren't you living at the compound anymore?"

Because she'd changed a lot at school. Despite needing her pack for support, she'd also found that she craved a little bit more freedom after having been on her own for the last four years. Instead of telling him that, she told a partial truth. "I'm getting my master's at Tulane, and I was worried it would be hard to study at the mansion."

He nodded. "I hear that. I've actually been talking with some of the guys about getting a place here in the Quarter. Be easier when we want to bring ladies home, you know?"

"God, you're such a horndog." She shook her head and nudged him with her hip. She might be twenty-three, but she felt light years more mature than Saul. "I see my friends. I'll talk to you later."

He grinned good-naturedly and resumed looking like a badass security guy as she walked toward the bar. Daphne could see Hector watching her intently, but she didn't turn in his direction. Her entire body flared to life when she realized he was aware of her. Heat blossomed low in her belly and she wanted to curse him for having that affect on her. It took self-control she didn't know she had, but she waved at the two human friends from one of her classes in the public health program without flicking him a single glance. Sydney and Annika smiled when they saw her.

Annika slid a full martini toward her as she reached their high-top table. "I ordered you one when I got your text saying you were on your way."

"Thanks." Taking off her fitted jacket she sat on the chair next to Sydney because it put her back to Hector. She could almost swear she felt his gaze on her, but wondered if that was her imagination.

"You know that hot bouncer?" Sydney asked, her dark eyes widening with interest.

"Um, yeah. Pretty much everyone who works here is part of my pack. But stay away from him. He's likely only interested in a booty call. And FYI, he can probably hear you." And that male likely didn't need his ego stroked even more.

Daphne held in a grin as she heard Saul curse. Her friends wouldn't be able to hear him, and normally she tuned most conversations going on around her out. It was like background noise. It was how she was managing to filter out whatever Hector was talking about with the female at his table on the other side of the bar.

"Crap, I totally forget you guys can do that." Sydney shook her head and took a sip of her drink.

Daphne did the same, but finished hers in a few swallows. She had a much higher metabolism and would have to drink four drinks to even feel any affect. Moments later, when Annika pulled her onto the dance floor, she found herself relaxing like she hadn't been able to since she'd moved back to New Orleans. As she swayed to a familiar remake of a song from a decade ago, she was almost able to tune out Hector's presence and the fact that she was pretty sure someone had been watching her for a month. It felt so good to just let go, to be free from responsibility for a little while. She'd killed herself taking a full load of classes every semester until she graduated with honors, and now she had two more years of school.

When the cover band started playing another familiar song, neither she nor her friends left the floor. She wasn't worried about her stuff at the table. This was a shifter run and owned bar. No one would mess with anything. Not unless they wanted an ass-kicking.

She wasn't sure how much time had passed, but over a dozen songs later the band took a break so she headed back to the table. Within seconds the girls were surrounded by males. Some shifters, some humans, and even a few vampires. It was Friday night and everyone was out looking for a good time.

As Annika and Sydney headed back to the dance floor with partners, Daphne begged off and motioned to one of the servers walking around. The second after the woman took her order, she scented a very familiar male near her. That fresh scent that had always reminded her of the rainforest was something she could pick out anywhere.

"Too good to say hi to me?" Hector's low voice wrapped around her as he sidled up to the table, looking sexy as hell. His coffee-colored hair was a little long on the sides, and he had that perfect bronze tan that he never had to work for. He pulled up one of the chairs and propped against it, not fully sitting, as if he wasn't sure he planned to stay. Wearing dark jeans that encased long, very muscular legs and a black sweater with the sleeves pushed up to his forearms, he looked delicious.

Daphne tried not to notice the way his muscles flexed as he crossed his arms over his chest, watching her curiously. His green eyes were mesmerizing and seemed more vivid against his tanned skin. She smiled brightly, hoping she didn't appear affected by him. "You looked busy and I didn't want to intrude."

His gaze narrowed on her lips, and for a moment, she could see a raw, hungry look in his eyes. He did it so quickly, but it made her stomach do annoying flips. He'd never looked at her like that before. "You think I'd ever be too busy for you?" The sincerity in his voice rolled over her like a soothing caress.

She swallowed hard and shrugged. "I figured you didn't want your sister's friend cramping your style."

He frowned in confusion as his gaze strayed behind her to where he'd been sitting. She didn't turn around because she didn't want to see the pretty redhead he'd been sitting with. Just as quickly his expression cleared. "That's Inez, my buddy Raul's mate. I was just keeping her company until he got here. They just moved from Costa Rica, and she doesn't know many people."

Daphne hated the relief that punched through her. She didn't care who Hector spent his time with. *Yeah, sure,* she told herself. "Oh." *Great response,* she chided herself.

"Leta told me you dropped by her place last week." His voice was so calming and open.

He might be insanely attractive, but he also went out of his way to make people feel at ease. It was one of the things she'd always adored about him. Even when she'd been younger he'd never made her feel bad when she and Leta had wanted to hang out with him, though she was pretty sure they'd gotten on his nerves.

Daphne nodded and marginally relaxed. Talking about Leta was a safe subject. "Yeah. I can't believe she's pregnant. She looks so adorable with her little bump. Are you excited to be an uncle?"

Hector smiled, a real one, and it took her breath away. Normally he only gave little half-smiles where one corner of his lip curved up. If he kept this up she'd be in a puddle of mush at his feet. "Yeah. She's gone a little crazy."

"Oh, I got to see the proof of that. It's good that some things never change." Daphne's friend had already bought the crib, painted the room a sage green, childproofed the toilets and cabinets—and she wasn't even three months along. Shifter pregnancies only lasted seven months, but it was still early to be worrying about that stuff. Leta had always been a little high strung, which had seemed so at odds with her chosen profession as an artist.

"I agree," he said softly, and she was under the impression he wasn't talking about his sister at all. He raked her with a gaze that sent chills skittering over her body and had her nipples tightening against her bra cups. He was clearly aware of her, probably seeing her as a woman for the first time. Which is what she'd wanted. But she didn't know what to do with the feelings bubbling up inside her. Before she could think of a response, he held out a hand. "Want to dance?"

The music had picked up as the band had started playing again. *Yes, no, yes, no.* The answers warred in her mind. Dancing with him would be a mistake, but—Hector slid his hand into hers, lightly linking their fingers together. He had a few calluses she'd never noticed before and the intimate way he was holding her hand made her decision.

She was definitely dancing with him. Letting him pull her onto the crowded dance floor, she didn't bother trying to keep her distance. She let her body press up against his lean, muscular one as they both moved in tune to the music. Daphne had never seen him dance before, and for some reason she was surprised by how well he did. He had a natural rhythm and the most primal part of her wondered if that would translate to the bedroom.

Even though he'd lived in New Orleans for almost a decade she'd never heard any chatter that he slept around. She knew he'd had lovers because she'd seen him out with a female once many years ago—and they'd clearly been more than friends—but he didn't have a reputation as a player. Hector kept things under wraps. He was a jaguar shifter and not part of any pride. He'd made his home here with Leta years ago, and taking care of her had always been his priority. Daphne was glad she'd never heard about him being a player because the thought of him hooking up with a bunch of women would carve her up inside.

Worried he'd read something in her expression, she turned her back to him and pressed into his body. She hadn't planned to, but it was instinctual. Her inner wolf wanted him wrapped around her in every way possible. He was tall, well over six feet, and lean in the way that most feline shifters were. All sleek muscles and hard lines. Feeling that against her body had her about to combust. He purred as his big hands settled on her hips and tugged her even closer to him. The feel of his erection against her lower back surprised her. He wasn't even trying to hide it. She'd seen the flicker of desire in his eyes when he'd approached her at the table, but to actually feel the proof was almost surreal. She was overheated and a little dizzy.

How the hell had she ever thought she could get this shifter out of her system? Her wolf hadn't been able to get over him in the time she'd been away at college. No one compared to him. Being so close to him was short-circuiting her ability to think straight. When the song ended, she stepped away from him and turned. Even though another song started, she pointed toward her table where Sydney was now sitting. "I should get back to my friend, but it was good seeing you, Hector. I'll talk to you later."

She felt guilty at his dejected expression, but she turned away and weaved through the growing throng of people toward her friend. She'd wanted him to notice her, but she hadn't expected such a blatant reaction from him. It had pushed her completely off-balance. If she kept dancing with him, she wouldn't want to stop. And that had disaster written all over it. She wasn't a freaking masochist. Hector might want her physically, but she knew that he wouldn't want anything long-term. He'd made that clear four years ago.

Chapter 2

Hector leaned against the front door frame as he talked to Saul. Too bad all his focus was on one extremely sexy female currently dancing with a lupine shifter from the Campbell pack. Hector knew the guy and even liked him. But right now he wanted to pummel him for touching Daphne.

Daphne who looked like walking sex. That dress should be fucking illegal. She was tall and thin, not really lean, just slim and almost delicate. She'd gotten her height from her father, who was Greek, but other than that, she'd taken the rest of her attributes from her Korean mother. Though he knew she was physically strong, there was something about her that made him want to pull her into his arms and take care of her.

Who was he kidding? He didn't want to take care of her. He wanted her in his bed, calling out his name as she climaxed. Plain and simple. Of course, nothing about his feelings for her had ever been simple. She'd always been around when Leta was in high school and he'd never thought about her in a sexual way until a few months after her eighteenth birthday. It was as if she'd blossomed overnight. But at ten years older than her, he'd felt like a lecher and avoided her at all costs—though his jaguar side hadn't understood what the hell his problem was.

Plus, she'd always had a crush on him and it would have been wrong for him to act on it, knowing how inexperienced she was. For a year his attraction had only grown to epic proportions.

Then he'd almost given in to kissing her at her nineteenth birthday party but stopped himself. She'd been drinking, and if he'd kissed her, he wouldn't have stopped at kissing. She wasn't the kind of woman to walk away from, and considering she was leaving for college, nothing good could have come from it. He knew he'd bruised her feelings back then, but that was a long time ago and she would have gotten over it, over him. Now she was home to stay, according to his sister.

And she wasn't too young anymore. She'd clearly grown up in more ways than one. He could see it in the confident way she walked and dressed. While he hated the thought of other men looking at her in that tight dress, he more than appreciated how she looked. That she was secure with who she was now.

"You've got it fucking bad." Saul's words made Hector glance over at his friend.

"Huh?" *Crap, had Saul been saying something?*

Saul shook his head. "I've been telling you about the gorgeous blonde over at the high-top tables undressing you with her eyes and you're staring at Daphne like you want to take her right on the bar."

The visual *that* evoked had his entire body tightening with need. The thought of her splayed out for him was almost too much. He knew Daphne had been aware of his erection when they'd danced. He'd felt like a randy cub when she'd pressed against him, but he hadn't bothered trying to hide it. What would be the point?

He wanted her to know he was affected because he wanted his desire for her clear. Then she'd walked away from him and he wasn't sure why. The sweet jasmine scent of her desire had teased him above everything else in the bar. It was clear she was attracted to him, but still she'd walked away. Maybe... she didn't feel the same pull he did. The thought made his jaguar snarl.

"You are so screwed," Saul murmured, but Hector continued ignoring him.

Hector knew the lupine shifter was right. He *was* screwed. Something primal had hit him in full force the second she'd walked into the bar. He couldn't know for sure, but it was like his body had awakened at seeing her. It was insane to think this was the mating call considering she was a wolf and he was a jaguar, but it wasn't impossible. There was no one singular sign; he'd always been told he'd just *know*. As if it was that simple.

As he watched the male lupine shifter she was dancing with move even closer, Hector almost lost control. He was known for being laid-back, but now his dominant nature was roaring to the surface. Not caring about the consequences, he stalked toward her. Weaving through the tables and ignoring anyone who spoke to him, he headed right for the dance floor.

Daphne looked over at him in surprise, and then something flickered across her features he couldn't define. Not fear exactly. God, he couldn't deal with it if she was ever afraid of him. But she was nervous.

Jessie, the man she was dancing with, slapped Hector's shoulder when he saw him. "Hey, man. How you doing?"

Hector couldn't look at him. He was afraid if he did, he'd do something he'd regret. His behavior was completely irrational, but he was okay with that. His inner jaguar was feeling possessive and he rarely fought his instincts. "Find a new dance partner," he growled before clasping Daphne's hips and pulling her close. Her dress was silky smooth against his fingers.

Jessie protested for half a second, but Hector completely tuned him out as Daphne moved into his arms, pressing her breasts against his chest.

If she'd resisted he would have let her go, but she melted against him, immediately linking her fingers behind his neck. The surprise on her face was evident, but it was clear she didn't mind what he'd done.

He loved how tall she was. Her body fit against his perfectly and as she swayed to the hypnotic beat, he could imagine how she would move on top of him. She'd pulled her long, straight black hair into a tight ponytail that showed off her sharp cheekbones. But he wanted to see her hair down, cascading around her as she rode him.

Even though she was holding on to him, she still eyed him with curiosity and a touch of nervousness. "Why did you do that?"

"I don't want anyone touching you but me." The admission surprised him even as he spoke the words, but he wouldn't take them back. It was the truth.

Her eyes widened and she opened her mouth once, but then her lips pulled into a half smile as if what he'd said pleased her. Closing her eyes, she moved in a sensuous rhythm against him. He was glad she didn't want to talk because he wasn't sure he could formulate any words at the moment. Not when she was pressed so close. Holding her like this calmed him in a way he didn't completely understand.

Song after song played and she never left his arms. A few other males from her pack had eyed her with obvious intent, but she'd latched on to him and ignored everyone else. That alone soothed his inner jaguar.

When the band eventually stopped playing, he was loath to release her. But the bar was closing in fifteen minutes and everyone would be clearing out soon. He walked her back to the table where her two friends were busy talking to two males. One human, one lupine shifter. Good, at least he wouldn't have a rapt audience in case she rejected him.

Daphne picked up her jacket, but instead of putting it on, she held it close to her chest, wrapping her arms around her body almost as if she was shielding herself from him. Her expression was shuttered and he couldn't get a read on her. That was like a jolt to his senses. He didn't want her pulling away from him.

"I want to see you again, Daphne." His voice sounded raspy and uneven. There was no way she could miss it.

She bit her bottom lip in the way she'd always done when she was nervous or unsure. "I don't know."

For a brief moment he wondered if she was playing games, but the sense he got from her was real. She seemed unsure of herself. Or maybe him.

"How about dinner tomorrow night?" He wanted to lock down a time and place with this sexy woman. Hector wasn't stupid. Half the males in the bar tonight had been checking her out. She'd just moved home and would have her pick of any man she wanted. He wanted that male to be him and he was willing to fight for her. She was one of the sweetest, most giving people he'd ever met.

"Um..."

"She'd love to," her blonde human friend said, a sly grin on her face.

Daphne gave her friend an annoyed glare, but she nodded at Hector. "I would. I don't live at the mansion anymore. I have my own place, so you can pick me up or I can meet you somewhere."

"I'll pick you up." That was a no-brainer. "Did you park close to here?" He knew she could take care of herself, but he didn't want her walking alone at night. Hell, he wasn't ready to say good-bye to her yet.

"I'm close enough." She gave him a tight smile as she slipped her jacket on. "You want to get my number from Leta tomorrow?"

Something about her tone bugged him. He wondered if she planned to blow him off. Shaking his head, he pulled out his own phone. "How about you give it to me now instead?" He wasn't going through his younger sister for anything.

When her lips pulled into a thin line, he realized he might be right. She rattled off her number and he texted her once he'd stored it.

"Now you have mine too," he said softly.

Her cheeks flushed a light shade of pink. "I'm going to say good-bye to some people, so I guess I'll talk to you tomorrow?"

Hating the wall she was erecting between them, he nodded and headed to the door of the bar. Once he was outside, he told his feet to move, but he leaned against the outside wall instead. His motorcycle was parked a block away and he was in no rush to get home. Not when he knew he wouldn't be able to sleep.

Half a dozen people spilled out from the double doors before Daphne finally made an appearance.

She nearly stumbled in her heeled boots when she saw him. "Hey."

"Hey, thought I'd walk you to your car."

There was such a vulnerable look in her dark eyes it made him frown, but she blocked it so quickly he could almost pretend he imagined it. "I didn't actually drive. I walked. I didn't say anything before because I knew you'd feel responsible."

"Responsible?" *What the hell was she talking about?*

She made a vague gesturing motion with her hand. "You know, because I'm Leta's friend."

He snorted, but ignored her statement and decided to go with distraction. "I got a new Ducati."

Immediately her arms dropped from around herself and she stepped closer to him, the excitement rolling off her in waves. Even if this was a different kind of excitement than the way she'd been turned on earlier when they were dancing, her jasmine scent teased him mercilessly. "You did *not*."

"I did." He grinned at the pleasure playing across her face. "Maybe I'll even let you drive it."

"You're such a liar. I remember begging you to drive your old Harley and it was always, 'when you're old enough.' " She laughed, the rich sound a balm to his senses.

This was the Daphne he remembered, relaxed and carefree. "You're definitely old enough now."

She sucked in a quick breath but held his gaze. There was so much heat there it stole his breath. She looked away first, scanning the street. "So where is it?"

"Let me drive you home and I'll show it to you." What he wouldn't give to feel her arms wrapped around him, her breasts pressed against his back...

"That sounds a lot like blackmail to me." Humor danced in her gaze.

"No, blackmail would be if I told you I'd let you drive it in exchange for a kiss." He had no idea why he was pushing when she'd made it clear in the bar that she needed some distance, but he couldn't help himself.

Her dark eyes widened and she nervously liked her lips, her pink tongue darting out in a way that was so sensual because she probably wasn't aware she'd done it. "You'd really let me drive your bike for a kiss? And not just for a measly block or two?"

"You can have it all day if you want. Do we have a deal?" He held back a grin as her jasmine scent intensified. She was definitely turned on and he hoped it was because of him, not his damn bike.

She shrugged. "Sure. A kiss is no big deal."

He nearly growled at her flippant words and stepped closer. When they did kiss, it would be a very big deal. He'd make sure of it.

Her eyes started to flutter closed as he leaned down, and though he desperately wanted to kiss her, to pull her close, he didn't. Moving until his mouth was a fraction from her earlobe, he whispered, "I didn't say it would be on your lips or how long it would last." Let her make of that what she wanted.

She swallowed hard and stepped back from him. While he definitely scented desire, he could tell that he'd pushed her enough for one night. Well, early morning as it was.

Needing to keep things relaxed between them, he nudged her with his shoulder playfully. Though he wanted to wrap his arm around her, he held off. "Come on, I'll drive you home. It has nothing to do with feeling responsible for you either. It's for purely selfish reasons. It'll make me feel better to know you're home safe."

"Hmm." She didn't say more after that. The click of her boots along the sidewalk as they walked and the sounds of other patrons stumbling home or hailing taxis filled the early morning hours.

A chill was in the air, causing his breath to curl in front of him like white smoke. They reached his bike in minutes, and when she let out a pleased groan at the sight of his ride, all he could envision was her making that sound as she rode him.

Though he wanted to let her drive so he could hold her from behind, a man could only take so much. Not trusting his voice, he slid on the front and looked back at her with raised eyebrows. Her dress was short so she'd have no problem getting on. It would also let anyone see a whole lot of leg not covered by those fuck-me boots, and while the thought of others looking at her grated on him, she was with *him*. At least for the length of the drive to her home.

As she slung one boot-clad leg over, he didn't bother biting back a groan. God, the woman was walking sex appeal. "What's the address?" he murmured.

After giving it to him, she asked, "No helmet?"

"Didn't know I'd have a riding partner tonight." But he planned to buy her one tomorrow.

Without responding, she slid her arms around him and pressed tight. Even through his sweater and her dress, the feel of her delicate body against his made him shudder. He could just imagine what it would be like to turn around and pull her into his lap so that she was straddling him and... On that note, he revved the engine and tore away from the curb. He needed to keep his shit together if he wanted a chance with her. Acting like a randy cub wasn't going to do him any favors.

The drive was a hell of a lot quicker than he'd anticipated. As he parked in front of the two-story brick townhome, his entire body was already mourning the loss of having to leave her. His reaction to her was so primal it terrified him. He'd only been in her presence for a few hours, but he felt as if he'd been sucker-punched and the effect just kept going.

"Thanks for the ride." Daphne was breathless as she got off the bike. "I can't wait until I get to drive it all by myself." Her grin was wicked.

It made him think of all the ways he wanted to pleasure her with his mouth. He started to respond when his jaguar senses went on full alert. Getting off the bike, he stood in front of Daphne and surveyed the street. There were cars and trucks parked along the curb, Mardi Gras beads hanging from trees that had been there for a hundred years, but he didn't see anyone. That didn't mean someone wasn't there, lurking in the shadows.

"You sense it too?" Daphne asked, her voice so low he almost didn't hear her.

He nodded and took a step back so that he was next to her. Wrapping his arm around her shoulders, he walked with her up the set of short stairs to the front door and stood guard while she unlocked it. She didn't argue with him when he came inside and did a full sweep of her place, which told him a lot. As an alpha shifter, Daphne knew how to take care of herself, but if she was letting him scan her home, she was nervous.

"Have you had problems with anyone lately?" he asked after checking all her rooms.

She paused for a moment, but shook her head. "No."

"What were you thinking of just then?"

She wrapped her arms around herself. "It's nothing tangible. Just a feeling I've been getting lately. Ever since I moved back, actually. Like I'm being watched. No one's approached me, though."

Someone or something was out there watching her right now. Hector could feel it to his core. After a brief hug and instructions to set her alarm, he let himself out. But he didn't go far.

Hell no.

He didn't tell her he planned to stick around just in case anyone with oversensitive hearing was listening. If someone was watching her, he was going to find out who they were and what their intentions were. And if they planned to hurt Daphne in any way, they were in for a surprise.

Chapter 3

After parking a few streets over from Daphne's, Hector raced through streets and yards until he reached the shotgun style house located directly behind her townhome. He couldn't scent anyone inside the home, but he was still careful as he crept along the side of the wood-paneled house and into the stranger's backyard. Using the shadows as cover, he was as silent in human form as he would have been as a jaguar.

He grasped the top of the high privacy fence and pulled himself up and over. He barely made a sound as he landed on the soft grass. Daphne's backyard was small, with a patio that held a table, chairs, and a charcoal grill. One live oak stood near the back fence and neatly trimmed bushes lined her home.

Pausing by the fence, Hector inhaled deeply. He never doubted his animal senses and right now they told him something wasn't right. A light in the top left window went on. He knew it was Daphne's bedroom from when he'd done a quick scan of the place. Her blinds were shut and he'd seen curtains pulled over those, so there was no way he'd get a glimpse of her.

Not that he should be thinking about that. He wanted to figure out what the hell he'd sensed earlier and keep her safe. Using lightning speed, he darted to the back patio then crept along the edge of her house until he rounded the corner. Crouching low, he didn't stop until he reached the front west side of her house. She didn't have any floodlights because she wouldn't need them with her extrasensory abilities. He was grateful for the extra cover of darkness.

He could hear her moving around inside, though the sounds were muted. It was as if she'd had extra insulation put in place, which wouldn't be out of the ordinary for her to have done in a semi-populated place like this. It was probably more for her hearing comfort than worrying about outsiders hearing her.

Hector tensed as a man with his hands shoved in his pockets and a hoodie pulled up over his head appeared from behind a wide oak tree across the street. Hector hadn't seen anyone walking or running from either direction, so either the guy had been waiting behind it for a while or he'd dropped from the branches. From his angle, Hector couldn't see the guy's face clearly, but when he strode across the street with purposeful, quick intent toward Daphne's place, Hector readied himself.

Letting his claws unsheathe, Hector waited until the male had reached the bottom of Daphne's stairs before he sprinted at him with full force.

The man cried out as Hector tackled and slammed him onto the ground. The hood fell back from the blond man's face and amber eyes glowed up at him. *Vampire.*

Hector pumped a fist into the guy's ribs and he cried out again. He struggled against him, trying to claw at Hector's face and sides, but his movements were erratic and clearly untrained. Ignoring the pain from a slash that ran along his upper arm, Hector wrapped a fist around the vamp's throat and dug his claws into his skin.

Using all his strength, he jumped up to his feet and dragged the vampire with him. He held him up in the air in a display of dominance and strength, wanting to make it clear that he was stronger than the other male. The vampire grabbed at his wrists and tried to free himself.

"It won't take much for me to kill you, little vamp," Hector growled, barely leashing his jaguar. "I'm going to ask this once. Why were you watching Daphne's house?"

When the man tried to answer, he only coughed and sputtered. Hector realized he needed to loosen his grip.

"Hector!" Daphne's footsteps pounding down the stairs behind him ricocheted into the cold night air. He didn't turn, not wanting to take his gaze off the threat in front of him.

Daphne placed a gentle hand on his forearm. "Let him go. I know him."

Instead of releasing his grip, Hector turned to face her. He knew his jaguar was likely showing in his eyes, but he couldn't help that. "You were expecting him at this hour?"

Jaw clenched, she shook her head and glared at him. "No. Not that it's any of your business if I *had* been expecting him. I could have been expecting a dozen guys—"

He snarled, the vicious noise cutting off her words and killing all sound around them. The thought of any male touching her, much less a dozen, had his inner cat going crazy. He'd locked away his feelings for her for years, pretended they didn't exist. That wasn't happening now. She was back in New Orleans and all grown up. He would be staking his claim very soon.

Looking away from her surprised face, he glared at the vampire still dangling in the air. "I'm letting you go. If you make a move toward her, I'll end your life."

With wide eyes, the blond nodded. The male sucked in a deep breath and stumbled as Hector dropped him. He looked back and forth between Hector and Daphne, fear rolling off him in waves. He shoved his hands in his jeans pockets and didn't take a step toward either of them.

Before Hector could speak, Daphne asked, "What the hell is going on, Troy? Why are you here? And when did you become a vampire?"

He shrugged, and for the first time since Hector had noticed the guy, he realized that he looked young. Maybe eighteen or nineteen. "I followed you from the shifter bar. I wanted to talk to you earlier, but you haven't been returning my phone calls. I didn't know if you'd want to see me."

"So you thought showing up at my house unannounced was the way to go?" Daphne's voice was scolding, but soft.

Way too soft for how she should be responding to this guy. Hector didn't understand why she was basically letting him off the hook.

Troy flicked a quick glance at Hector then looked back at Daphne. "Is this your new boyfriend? Is that why you're not returning my calls?" There was no hiding the disgust in his voice.

What the hell? Did she actually date this guy?

Daphne sighed. "My personal life is none of your business—something we have discussed. You need to leave. It's early and I'm sure you need to get back to wherever you're staying before sunrise. I'll call you tomorrow night and we'll talk, but you can't do this again. If you show up at my home or my school or do anything like this again, I'll file a restraining order against you and have my Alpha call whoever made you. My Alpha is *not* the forgiving type. You know the kind of consequences you'll be dealing with, don't you?"

When Troy nodded and sprinted away without another word, Hector let out a frustrated breath. "What the hell, Daphne?"

She sighed and nodded toward her house. "Have time for a cup of coffee?"

Yeah, like he was leaving. After scanning the neighborhood again, he followed her inside. Her natural jasmine scent was stronger here and it enveloped him as he strode toward her kitchen. Though he'd seen the inside of her home earlier, he'd been focused on finding a threat. Now he could appreciate all the small touches that showed Daphne's influence. Even though the kitchen was sleek and modern, there were fresh flowers on the kitchen table and four little plants on the windowsill that overlooked the backyard.

"Forget the coffee. Who the hell is that guy and why did you let him go?" Hector leaned against the counter by the sink as she collapsed onto one of the stools by the marble-topped island.

Daphne scrubbed a hand over her face. She wasn't wearing her boots anymore, just pink bunny slippers that gave her an adorable, almost innocent quality. "My senior year I did some tutoring and he was one of my students. He's not a bad kid, just really confused and messed up. Troy comes from a broken home with no mother and he developed this... obsession with me. At first it was just phone calls. He started calling me with clearly made up issues about his homework. But then he started calling at all hours of the night wanting to know who I was with and what I was doing.

"He thought I wouldn't date him because I was his tutor, so he found another one. Then he somehow came to the conclusion that it was because I was a shifter and he was human and our life spans were too different. I was fine to let him think that. I finally stopped returning his calls because I realized nothing I said would make a difference. Then he started showing up outside my classes or waiting for me in the school parking lot by my car. When I graduated and moved I thought it would be the end of it. He's just a human so I wasn't really worried about him, but..." She trailed off and looked down at her clasped hands which were clenched tightly in her lap. "I can't believe he followed me here. What if he turned vampire because of me?"

"You need to tell Angus," Hector said quietly.

Her head snapped up and her dark eyes were conflicted. "If I do, you know what will happen."

Hector nodded. As she'd suggested, Angus was definitely not the forgiving type. He meted out punishment with the kind of harsh brutality one would expect from a three-hundred-year-old Alpha who'd managed to maintain control of the New Orleans territory for as long as he had. And Daphne was a favorite among her pack. Angus and his mate, Iris, were close to Daphne's parents. This would not go over well at all. "This guy is *stalking* you, Daphne. You get that, don't you?"

"Of course I get it. I just don't want him to get hurt. I feel bad for him." Unshed tears glistened in her eyes as she looked away from him.

Oh, hell. Covering the distance between them, Hector pulled her off the stool and gathered her in his arms. Without her boots she was a little shorter and her face fit right against his chest.

She sniffled a little and wrapped her arms around him, holding him tight. "You probably think I'm being stupid for being worried about what happens to him," she muttered.

He sighed. "No, I think you have a big heart." That didn't mean Hector had to be magnanimous toward the guy. He planned to find out everything he could about the human-turned-vampire and make sure he stayed the hell away from Daphne.

After a few minutes she pulled away from him and wiped at her eyes. "Thanks for listening. I'm sorry you even have—"

He shook his head. "Stop. I'm not sorry. You clearly needed to tell someone about this. It doesn't matter that you're a shifter and he's a human—well, a vamp, now. Being stalked isn't something anyone should have to deal with, let alone deal with by themselves. And you haven't told anyone, have you?"

Flushing guiltily, she shook her head.

He was pissed she'd been keeping this to herself, but scolding her wouldn't get him anywhere. She'd just been trying to handle it in her own way. "Come on. I'm sleeping in the guest room and I know you must be beat." He didn't bother asking if he could stay over because leaving wasn't an option.

For a brief moment it looked as if she might argue, but she just sighed and turned toward the entryway. "All right. I'll get you some extra towels in case you want to take a shower."

Chapter 4

Daphne lifted her face up to the pulsing jets of her shower, savoring the feel of the heat cascading over her body. She was beyond stunned that Troy had shown up at her townhome. Even more so that he was now a vampire. The last couple months at school she'd almost felt like a prisoner, trying to hide from him all the time. She'd been so sure that when she returned home she'd be leaving that problem behind her. Maybe she should have done things differently.

Deep down she was terrified that she'd somehow led him on or given him a mixed signal in some way. She'd always kept things professional but maybe . . . Oh, hell, who knew? The truth was, she wasn't responsible for his actions and she was just making herself crazy.

After turning off the shower, she wrung the water from her hair before wrapping herself in a big fluffy towel. The shower had helped somewhat and now all she wanted to do was sleep and forget about Troy.

She really hated that Hector was even aware of any of this. It was so embarrassing. She could take care of herself and didn't want him to view her as some kid. She'd just never thought she'd have to deal with a stalker. That was something that happened to celebrities. Once she'd brushed her teeth and twisted her wet hair up into a clip, she eased the door open and stepped into her bedroom.

Hector was sleeping in the next room, but shifter hearing was keen and she didn't want to disturb him. It was sweet that he was staying over even if it did make her feel like he was trying to take responsibility for her. She didn't want a babysitter or bodyguard. She wanted him as a lover—her first real one.

And she didn't want him to think of her as his sister's friend or someone he needed to look out for, but as a woman. She wanted to feel his body over hers and—she let out a yelp as she ran into the trunk she'd pulled down earlier from her walk-in closet.

Her bedroom door flew open. Hector stepped into her room, claws unsheathed, his jaguar clear in his gaze. Blinking, he scanned the room then focused on her. His eyes quickly turned full human as he retracted his claws. "Are you okay?" he rasped out.

"Yeah, I just… why aren't you in bed?" He might be fast, but there was no way he'd made it from the guestroom to hers that quickly.

He shrugged and a spicy, pure masculine scent rolled off him as he stared at her.

She realized he'd likely been sitting or lying outside her room. She narrowed her gaze. "You don't need to stand guard outside the whole night. I'm a shifter too and completely capable of taking care of myself."

"I know. But that doesn't change the fact that I want to take care of you too," he said quietly.

Oh. Daphne struggled to find the right words, any words, but he continued.

"I think it's time for that kiss." His gaze traveled over her body in a lazy path of unabashed admiration.

She was wearing a towel, but the way his gaze was blazing a trail from her head down to her pink toenails made her feel completely bared to him. If she was braver, she'd drop the towel, but there was no way she could do that. As a shifter, she was comfortable with her body and nudity, but Hector had never seen her naked and it would definitely change things between them if he did. Especially if she dropped her towel and he wasn't interested. That thought doused some of her lust.

Hector frowned at her as he stepped farther into the room. "What are you thinking?"

She shook her head. "Nothing."

His eyes narrowed and he walked toward her until they were inches apart. Nervously she licked her lips and felt a small jump inside her belly when his gaze zeroed in on her mouth. She'd fantasized about what it would be like to kiss him, but now that she was faced with the reality, she knew it would be better. Had no doubt in her mind.

"Lie on the bed," he whispered.

It took a moment for his words to sink in. "What?"

"Now." There was a commanding edge to his voice that took her off guard, mainly because she really liked it.

Daphne didn't know if she should keep her towel on or what kind of kiss required her to lie down, but she did as he said. Anticipation and desire hummed through her in equal measures.

Hector stood at the end of the bed, tall and intimidating, and without his sweater on, sexy as sin. She'd noticed his chest when he'd walked in—she'd have to be blind not to—but as she let her eyes travel over all those hard, muscular planes her belly tightened with need.

Without a word Hector kneeled on the bed, never taking his gaze from hers. His green eyes were smoldering and practically electric as he watched her. He gently took one of her ankles and lifted it toward his mouth.

She might be wearing a towel, but the position would give him a perfect view of everything underneath it. Instead of kissing her ankle, like she'd expected, he gently ran his nose over her skin, inhaling slightly, as if he couldn't get enough of her.

God, just watching him holding her leg was turning her on. Her inner walls clenched involuntarily, and even though there was no way possible he could have known, his eyes narrowed a fraction. Had he scented her desire? *Of course he had.*

Scooting farther up on the bed, he inched closer to her, forcing her thighs to spread wider. When they did, her towel pushed up higher on her thighs. She made a move to hold it back down, but he just shook his head.

The thought of him being a demanding lover was so deliciously erotic. He would take, but she knew he'd be giving. Still holding her ankle, he continued his path up her leg, never touching her with his mouth. Never kissing her.

By the time he reached her inner thighs, she was practically quivering with excitement and yes, a lot of nervousness. Hector had already bypassed everything she thought he planned on doing. She was pretty sure he didn't want a quick fling, but she was also sure that it wouldn't last forever. Even though she figured she'd probably get her heart ripped out when things ended, there was no way she would stop things between them. No way in hell. She wanted everything he had to give. She'd been thinking about this, about him, for years. She wouldn't run away from this opportunity.

"Open your towel," he said softly, just a touch of a growl in his voice.

Her hands stilled at the top of it as a very short-lived war waged inside her. She wasn't a coward. She wanted this. Wanted Hector like she'd never wanted anyone. With slightly trembling hands, she pulled the towel free from where it was cinched above her breasts and exposed herself to him.

He swallowed hard, the lust blazing in his eyes going a long way to easing her panic. "Fuck, you're gorgeous," he murmured, almost to himself.

His words took away the rest of her lingering nervousness. "So where's my kiss?" She had no idea where she found the courage to ask, but his gaze snapped up to hers and she couldn't stop the grin that spread across her face.

His answering smile was positively wicked. Slowly, he slid his strong hands along her inner thighs until he reached the very top of them. He pressed on her legs so that she had no choice but to fully open herself to him.

Before she had a chance to be self-conscious, he leaned down and kissed her clit. Crying out in surprise, she jerked against his face, unable to stop herself. She'd thought she'd be more self-conscious but feeling his lips on her sensitive bundle of nerves was better than anything she could have fantasized about.

His tongue lazily stroked around her pulsing bud and the moans he made as he teased her lit her on fire. Slowly, he ran his tongue down her wet slit, then back up, centering on her clit again. She threaded her fingers through his hair, holding him to her when he abruptly stopped.

Panting, she stared at him. His green eyes glinted wickedly. "That's one kiss. Should I stop?"

She shook her head.

"Say it," he ordered.

More heat flooded between her legs. She could definitely get used to this dominating side of Hector. "Kiss me."

His lips quirked up. "That'll do for now," he murmured before he bent his head to her again.

The moment his lips and tongue made contact with her sensitive flesh, she knew it wouldn't take her long. She was so hot and primed for him she was ready to topple over the edge.

He surprised her by sliding two fingers inside her. The movement was smooth and unhurried and a sharp climax surged through her the moment he entered her. He didn't let up with his tongue though. He kept teasing and licking her as he slowly drew his fingers out of her. Her inner walls clenched wildly, needing to be filled by him. As if he knew what she craved, he pushed back in again, faster this time. He kept repeating it as her orgasm rolled through her. It seemed to go on forever as ribbons of pleasure punched out to all her nerve endings. After an eternity, she called out his name before collapsing in a boneless heap against the silky covers. She didn't care if she sounded desperate for him. At that moment, she was.

With heavy lidded eyes, she looked down at Hector. He looked so very male and so satisfied in that moment. She wanted to pull him to her, but she was soaking up the bliss of her climax and couldn't move.

Hector practically stalked up her body until his hands were on either side of her head, caging her in. She looped her legs around him, pulling his hard length flush against her. Even with his pants on, there was no denying he was *very* affected.

Leaning down, he covered her mouth with his. She could taste herself on him and couldn't believe how erotic that was. Tunneling her fingers through his hair, she clutched on to him, savoring the way he was kissing her with complete dominance. She could feel how tense he was, as if he was trying to control himself. His untamed energy was radiating off him.

He cupped her breast with one hand and began slowly strumming her nipple with his thumb. But as she arched into him, he pulled back and basically jumped off the bed.

Feeling hurt and vulnerable, she yanked her towel closed.

Before she could say anything, he gave a sharp shake of his head and spoke. "I don't want to rush this with you, Daphne. And I'm ready to take you right here. I can't keep touching you, but not because I don't want to. I do. Probably too much." His words came out choppy and uneven.

Clutching her towel tightly against her chest, she fought the awkwardness that was threatening to overtake her. "That was some first kiss." Her words immediately eased the tension in the room.

"I'm glad you think so." Hector grinned and strode to one of her antique dressers. "What do you normally sleep in?"

She really wanted to ask if he wanted a release in return, but she was too shy to ask. Her sexual experience was very limited and this was Hector in her bedroom. Something she'd only fantasized about. The words hovered on the tip of her tongue, but she couldn't push them out. Instead, she answered his question. "Naked or in a T-shirt. They're in the top drawer."

He pulled out a black T-shirt with a scene from the movie *The Crow* on it. It had been his years ago, but she'd taken it because she'd loved his scent. He brought the shirt to her and sat on the edge of the bed, clearly keeping distance between them. "This looks familiar," he said softly.

"I'm not giving it back," she said as she tugged it over her head and threw the towel on the floor.

Once she was dressed, they stared at each other for a long moment and she could tell he wasn't sure what to say either. She bit her bottom lip and he scooted a few inches closer.

He didn't touch her as he spoke. "I'd like to stay with you tonight. I'll keep my clothes on and—"

"Okay." She didn't even need to think about it. She wanted Hector's arms around her even if it would be a little bit of torture to be wrapped up in his strength and spicy scent.

She pulled her covers back and they slid in together. She turned her back to him and let him spoon her from behind as if they'd done it a thousand times. She could feel his erection against her back, but he just held her. Having him hold her like this was better than her fantasies. She couldn't believe that Hector was actually in bed with her. For the first time in so long she finally felt safe and able to sleep peacefully. No one would be getting past Hector.

Chapter 5

Daphne opened her eyes to the scent of bacon and coffee. Rolling over in her bed, she saw Hector was gone but knew he had to be the source of the delicious smells. After brushing her teeth and washing her face, she found him downstairs sitting at her kitchen table reading a newspaper and sipping coffee.

He looked so domestic it made her giggle.

His eyebrows rose. "What's funny?"

She shook her head and zeroed in on the full pot of coffee. Until she had coffee, she wasn't talking. There were strips of bacon on a plate next to the pot and a carton of eggs he'd laid out. She snagged a piece of bacon and bit into it. *Heaven.* She quickly poured a cup then sat at the table across from him. She definitely wasn't surprised he'd made himself at home. They'd known each other far too long for him to act otherwise. "How long have you been up?" Her voice was still scratchy from sleep.

"About an hour. Didn't have the heart to wake you." He raked a heated gaze over her face that told her he'd struggled with it, though.

She knew that being woken by him would be a sensual experience. Somehow she shoved that thought aside. "Thanks for breakfast and coffee. How'd you sleep?"

He gave her a hooded look that said so many things, yet nothing at all. He cleared his throat. "Well enough."

In other words, he would have slept better if they'd gotten more physical. Or she assumed that's what he was implying. Her insides were all twisted up around him. But she couldn't dwell on any of that right now. She had more important things to deal with. She needed to tell her Alpha what was going on with Troy, but didn't know how to broach the subject.

As if he read her mind, Hector's eyes narrowed. "You're going to tell Angus?"

Damn him for being so perceptive. "Yes, but I'm going to talk to Troy first. I told him I'd call him tonight and I'm going to. I'll tell him that I'm taking the situation to my Alpha. Maybe he'll just leave town when he hears that."

Hector grunted and stood. "How do you want your eggs?"

Okay then. Not up for discussion apparently. "Over easy. And I'd like three please." As a shifter she had a higher than normal metabolism and she was starving this morning. Glancing at the clock she saw that it was later than she'd realized. That orgasm had seriously knocked her out. "If you have to go to work in a few hours, don't feel like you have to stay."

Hector looked at her over his shoulder from where he stood in front of the stove. His green eyes were shuttered and she couldn't read the look he gave her. Finally he turned back around. An awkward silence stretched between them until he spoke.

"I took the day off. I'd like to spend it with you." Though he didn't form it as a question, she heard it in his words.

Daphne wondered if she was being stupid by getting tangled up with him. Really, where could this lead? Still . . . "Me too."

It was subtle, but the tenseness in his shoulders loosened. Shoulders that were unfortunately covered by his sweater. She'd been hoping for another peek at his chest and back. She started to ask if he had anything specific in mind when her landline rang. There were only two people who called her house. She picked up the portable from the cradle next to her refrigerator and inwardly cringed when she saw the number.

Not because she didn't want to talk to Leta, but because she'd just gotten intimate with her best friend's brother. Trying to act casual, she answered, "Hey."

"Hey. It's not too early is it?" Leta sounded panicked.

"Of course not. What's going on?" Forgetting her previous nervousness, she sat back at the table, keeping an eye on Hector.

"It could be nothing, but... two pregnant felines have gone missing in the last couple days. They don't have an Alpha to look out for them, and maybe I'm being silly, but I'm worried. I'm pregnant too and what if someone is targeting us?" Leta's voice rose with each word, the worry practically rolling off her through the phone line.

"What does your mate say?" Daphne asked, trying to keep her voice soothing. The thought of anyone targeting pregnant shifters was despicable. But pregnant shifters were almost as weak as humans and would be easy targets. What would be the point, though? She nearly snorted at herself before the thought had fully formed. There were enough hate groups that loathed supernatural beings that they wouldn't need a reason. Still, targeting pregnant women was pretty damn extreme.

"He wants us to be more cautious and he wants to get the word out to all pregnant shifters that something might be going on. I know there are some expectant moms in your pack, but you have an Alpha and..." Leta trailed off and Daphne could hear her sniffling.

"Oh, honey. Don't cry. I'll talk to my Alpha today and—"

"I've already talked to Angus about this," Hector said, cutting her off.

Daphne looked up from where she sat at the coffee table. He would have easily heard their phone conversation. "You did?"

He nodded. "Last night. I received a few frantic phone calls so I called him. He's promised to look into it, and you know Angus."

Daphne nodded. She did indeed. Her Alpha was extremely protective of those who lived in his city, regardless of species. If anyone fucked with supernatural beings in New Orleans, they'd be facing his wrath. "Did you hear that?" she asked Leta.

There was a long silence, then, "Yes." Leta cleared her throat, all traces of sniffling and crying gone. "Is that Hector?" Leta whispered, though there was no point considering Hector would definitely hear.

Daphne winced. It might be later than she normally slept in, but it was still only eight o'clock. There was no reason Hector would have stopped by this early and besides, she didn't plan to lie to her friend. "Yes."

"Go upstairs or somewhere private. I want to talk to you without my nosy brother listening."

Daphne glanced at Hector who just raised his eyebrows and shrugged. She hurried upstairs and ducked into her bathroom. She turned on the shower for extra noise. It should keep him from listening, though she had a feeling he was respectful enough to tune them out anyway. It was just the way Hector was.

"All right. I'm upstairs."

"Oh my gosh! Are you sleeping with my brother?" Leta didn't sound angry, which was a good sign.

"Not... exactly." She and Leta normally told each other everything, but there was no way she could tell her friend about last night.

"But you're... ah, I can't even say the words, but you're like, maybe hooking up with him?"

Daphne swallowed hard. "I have no idea what we are. You're not mad, though?"

"No! If you two get mated we'll finally be sisters for real."

"I seriously doubt—"

"Whatever, I don't want to hear it. I know you've always had a crush on him and let's just say he was very aware of you a few years ago."

Daphne snorted because that simply wasn't true, but she didn't comment. The one time she'd put herself out there for Hector, he'd rejected her attempt to kiss him. It had been humiliating, mainly because he'd tried to let her down gently. He'd been all sweet about it. If he'd been an asshole it would have been so easy to get over him. Ugh, she didn't even want to think about that. "Can we please not talk about Hector?"

Leta sighed dramatically. "Fine. But if you guys do get mated, I better be the first to know. That's all I want to know though. I don't want any details about... the rest of what you two do."

Daphne grinned. "No problem."

They talked for a few more minutes, mainly about Leta's fear for pregnant shifters, then disconnected. Leta had a very caring and dedicated mate, so Daphne wasn't worried about him watching out for her. Daphne was really glad Hector had already talked to her Alpha, but she planned to talk to Angus too about the Troy situation and the missing felines.

A few minutes later she found Hector downstairs putting both their plates on the table. Seeing him moving around her kitchen felt natural, like he belonged there. Not the kitchen exactly, but her house and her life. When he saw her, his gaze darkened and he quickly closed the distance between them. Before she could blink, he'd slid his fingers through her hair and clasped the back of her neck. His mouth brushed over hers, sensual and soft at first before developing into something needier.

He came at her hard, the strokes of his tongue demanding and hungry. She clutched at his shoulders, afraid she'd melt into a puddle at his feet. Her nipples tightened and unbearable heat flooded between her legs. The scent of her own desire intermingled with his and she was glad she wasn't the only one affected.

Eventually he pulled back, his breathing shallow. "After we eat, I was hoping we could spend the day at the Square."

She blinked, trying to absorb his words. It was amazing he could even talk after that kiss.

"You can drive my bike," he continued.

Okay, that jerked her out of her daze. The thought of driving his Ducati around the city and hanging out at Jackson Square was very appealing. "I might never give her back once you hand over the keys," she said as she sat at the kitchen table, proud of the way she kept her voice from shaking.

"Her?" He frowned as he sat across from her.

"Oh, yeah. That Ducati is definitely a she. In fact, I think I'm going to name her."

"Don't get too attached," he grumbled good-naturedly, a smile tugging at the corner of his lips.

Daphne couldn't help but wonder if there was a double meaning to his words. Don't get too attached to the bike or to him?

Chapter 6

Hector watched Daphne across the small table eating, trying not to stare too hard or to look like a lovesick cub. Even if that was exactly what he felt like. They'd spent the entire day at the Square, walking, shopping, and even taking a historical carriage ride. They'd known everything the guide had been telling them since they'd both lived there for years, but it had been touristy and relaxing. And it had let Hector hold her hand.

Such a small thing, but he liked touching her any way she'd let him. Daphne had been open and relaxed with him all day and he'd taken full advantage. She'd even bought him a voodoo doll at one of the local shops, telling him he should use it on annoying customers. Normally shopping was the last thing he wanted to do, but being with Daphne had been fun. Luckily there hadn't been any sign of that little shit, Troy. Hector was still angry about that vampire, and even though the guy was weaker than him, Hector didn't like to underestimate anyone. Even humans. It was a mistake.

"Want some of my po'boy?" Daphne held out her shrimp sub.

He shook his head and stabbed one of the fried shrimp on his plate with his fork. They'd stopped at a local restaurant on Iberville that he frequented at least once a week. The place was packed, but all his focus was on her. His inner jaguar and his human side were in complete accordance about her. He wanted to claim her, to make her his forever. Something his jaguar had known for longer than he wanted to admit.

"You sure? Because you're staring at it like you want to devour it." She held it out playfully.

Hector shook his head again. "It's not the po'boy I'm staring at." Not exactly subtle, but he couldn't stop himself. Daphne needed to know how serious he was about her. He was going to take things slow physically, but he didn't want there to be any doubt of his intentions.

Her cheeks flushed crimson and she mumbled something under her breath before taking a bite of her sub. The way she turned red was cute, but he was still unsure what she wanted from him. She'd been sweet and flirty, and yes, sensual all day, but he couldn't get a read on her.

"So what do you plan to do once you have your master's?" he asked after a few minutes.

Her eyes lit up as she set her food down. "I hope to get a job at the local VA. Veterans need better access to health care, not just here but on a national level. Eventually I'd like to get my PhD too, but I'm ready to start working as soon as I complete my master's."

She was right about the lack of good health care for veterans and he respected her for wanting to help. "What happens if you don't find a job locally? Will you leave?" They might not be even close to that place in their relationship, but if she needed to relocate, he knew he'd go anywhere she wanted. That knowledge alone told him how much he'd already fallen for her. It was likely too soon, but it felt like he'd known her forever. When she'd walked back into his life, something inside him had woken up with a vengeance. He'd felt the trickle of these feelings when she'd been nineteen and about to head to college. He'd ignored them, knowing the time wasn't right for her. Now, those feelings were full blown and they weren't going away. Ever. This female was it for him.

Daphne shook her head. "I honestly don't think that'll be a problem. I sort of have a standing job offer, but if something falls through then no, I'm not leaving again. I missed my pack and my family while I was at Duke. I'm glad I went away for college, but this is where I belong."

He was glad to hear it. Not that he wouldn't move for her, but he loved New Orleans. When he and Leta had moved there, he'd felt at home for the first time in his life.

"What about you?" she continued. "I know you don't plan to work for Angus forever."

"In the next five years I hope to open up my own restaurant in the Quarter, but I'm not in a rush. When I do it, I'm going to do it right." Restaurants and bars had a high failure rate. He knew that no matter how much he planned it still might not fly, but that didn't mean he wouldn't be as prepared as he could be.

"You know I love talking about food. What kind of restaurant?" She picked her sub back up and took another bite.

"A mix of South American and Creole food mainly, but I also plan to have a full bar and dance area. It will cater to humans or shifters during the daylight hours but all supernatural beings at night." Even though they were always welcome, Angus didn't cater to vampires at his bar and Hector wanted something all-inclusive. Vamps could spend some serious money and he had no problem capitalizing on that as long as everyone played nice.

"You'll be successful." Daphne said it so matter-of-factly, it took him off guard.

He'd never had a desire to go to college and he'd secretly wondered if that would be an issue with her. The fact that she believed in him warmed him from the inside out. "Yeah?"

She nodded. "Yeah. I've seen you at the bar and you pretty much run the place when Angus isn't around. You're a feline and I know he doesn't care about species differences, but still, that says a lot about how much he trusts you considering you're not technically pack. You think he'd ever let Saul run the place while he was gone?" Daphne rolled her eyes.

Hector didn't bother to fight his grin. He loved working with Saul, but the guy was too busy chasing tail to take anything seriously. Actually, all the lupine shifters that worked there were just as bad. "Good point."

Daphne started to say something when a member of her pack waved at them from across the restaurant. Hector nodded at the lupine shifter, Neil, as he approached. The wolf was tall, barely an inch shorter than Hector and he was broad. He was definitely an alpha in nature, but he wasn't a warrior member of the Campbell pack. He was also the same age as Daphne, and considering the way the dark-haired wolf was eyeing her, Hector had no doubt he was interested in her.

Keeping his jaguar contained would be harder than he'd expected because at that moment, he knew his cat was in his eyes. He knew because Daphne's eyes widened when she looked at him, but Neil had barely glanced at him once. If he had, he'd probably be backing the fuck off right now.

Neil shoved his hands in his pockets, as if he was nervous. The slightly bitter scent that rolled off him confirmed it. "Hey, Daphne. Heard you were back in town. You're staying, right?"

She nodded politely. "Yes, not at the mansion though. I've got my own place."

"Yeah, me too. Moved in with some of my brothers a month ago. I love the compound, but we needed some space. So, uh, I know you haven't been back long, but, uh, I was wondering if you'd like to have dinner with me sometime next week." The words came out in a rush, as if he'd been practicing.

Hector wanted to claw the little punk to shreds for asking her out right in front of him, but Daphne beat him to it. "Are you kidding me, Neil? I'm on a date right now. That's extremely rude to me and to Hector."

Damn, she didn't pull her punches. His jaguar smiled at her direct-ness.

Neil's eyes grew wide as his head snapped in Hector's direction. When he made eye contact, he took a step back. "Shit. Sorry, man. I thought you were Leta's brother."

"I am." Hector was surprised he'd managed to squeeze those two words out.

"Oh... I just assumed you guys were friends because of Leta. I didn't know... Sorry, sorry," he repeated as he backed away.

The only thing that made Hector feel a little bad for the guy was how red his face and ears had turned as he mumbled a good-bye and practically ran from the restaurant.

"Sorry about that," Daphne murmured as she picked her sub back up. She said it so casually, as if this was an everyday occurrence and he figured it was. She probably got hit on all the time, something his jaguar didn't like at all.

"You don't have anything to apologize for." Hector shrugged even though he felt anything but relaxed. He knew Daphne would be pursued by members of her pack and his human side understood why. She was gorgeous and at the prime age to mate. His animal side was just plain pissed that other males wanted her. And until—or if—they were mated, there wasn't a damn thing he could do about it.

Once they finished their meal, he paid and they made their way to his Ducati. She'd been driving it all day and he had to admit it was hot watching her slide onto it. With Daphne's long legs and lithe form, she looked so damn graceful.

A few blocks later she palmed the keys and swung them around her fingers once. "I feel like there was no losing that bet for me. I get to drive your ride and…" She trailed off and flushed, but he knew what she was thinking.

He leaned against her until she had to sit on the bike. Holding onto the handlebars, he embraced her with his body and didn't stop until his lips lightly brushed against hers. "And?"

"And I had the best orgasm of my life," she whispered.

Her words sent a jolt straight to his cock, which had been in a perpetual state of hell all day. Just being around her kept him aroused. The best orgasm? Hell, they were only just getting started. "Let's get out of here," he growled.

She nodded, her dark eyes glinting wickedly. He tried to tell himself that he'd show restraint tonight no matter what, but wondered if he was fooling himself. He'd never wanted a female so badly in his life. And he'd been celibate for *years*. The need to mate and claim her was almost overwhelming him.

Turning, she slid onto the bike and he got on behind her. His erection pressed up against her, but there was no helping that. Having Daphne in front of him like this brought up so many vivid and erotic fantasies. He'd love to take her from behind and sink his canines into her as they made love. The thought of bonding and mating with her didn't scare him at all.

After checking to make sure they were clear—Daphne was very careful with his bike—she pulled into traffic and zoomed away. She was a fast but aware driver, and as she zipped through traffic, he tightened his grip on her hips. He loved feeling her body against his in a way that floored him.

They were only two blocks from her home and the need and energy pulsing through him really made him wonder how the hell he'd be able to take things slow. They'd never talked about him staying over again, but he wanted to if she'd let him. And if she let him into her bed— *Fuck!*

Hector's head snapped up at the sound of screeching tires. A black SUV had pulled in from the oncoming lane of traffic and was gunning right at them.

They were going to be hit head-on in two seconds. He tensed, wrapping his arms around Daphne and wishing he could completely protect her, but she violently swerved.

They made a hard right and slammed into the curb. The turn was too sharp and the bike caught on the edge, throwing them forward. He tried to hold on to her but the impact was too much. He flew through the air over the sidewalk and slammed into a tree before bouncing back onto the pavement.

Pain ricocheted through his entire body and he was pretty sure he'd cracked a rib, but he jumped to his feet. The SUV was squealing away, but all he could focus on was Daphne's unmoving body sprawled face down in a patch of grass before him.

Panic humming through him, he raced toward her.

Chapter 7

With his heart in his throat, Hector slowly rolled Daphne over onto her back. When she blinked at him, some of his tension eased. Being a shifter made her incredibly strong and resilient, but seeing her lying motionless had ripped his heart out.

"I'm sorry about your bike," she said, her voice raspy.

An invisible fist tightened around his heart. "Fuck the bike. Are you okay? Is anything broken?"

Pushing herself up so that she was sitting, she stretched her arms out in front of her and moved her legs. "I'm good." Glancing up and down the sidewalk, she frowned. There weren't any humans walking by and a few people had tried to stop but the road was too narrow with no curbside parking. So the drivers had moved on after others honked incessantly. "Pissed, though. What was that jerk thinking?"

Hector wasn't sure it had been an accident. Before he could voice that thought, Daphne looked at him with concern etched on her face. She gently cupped his cheek. "Are you okay?" She ran her hands down his shoulders and arms, as if inspecting him for injuries.

He'd been in worse situations, but he liked the concern she was showing. "I'm fine." Unable to stop himself, he gathered her in his arms, hugging her close. Inhaling her jasmine scent soothed his raging inner jaguar. Someone had tried to hurt Daphne and that wouldn't go unpunished.

After a few long moments, she pushed at his chest. "You're going to suffocate me." Her voice came out garbled.

Though he didn't want to let her go, he wanted to get her the hell out of there. "Let's get you home."

As they both stood, his gaze on Daphne, she winced at the bike. It was on its side, scratched up, and the front light was busted. When her dark gaze met his, he could read what she was going to say before she did. "You don't think Troy was behind this, do you?"

The thought had definitely crossed Hector's mind. He hadn't scented the vampire while they'd been out today, but they'd also been in the heart of New Orleans where it was sometimes difficult to decipher everything. The perfect place to blend in if you were a supernatural being. "What does he drive?"

"I have no idea." She shook her head as she wrapped her arms around herself. Her sweater sleeves were torn and he could see traces of blood, but no injuries because she would have already healed.

"We're going to see Angus at the crack of dawn tomorrow." He wanted to take her tonight, but Daphne looked shaken up and so vulnerable. He wouldn't add to any of her stress.

She nodded once. "Okay."

"And I'm staying over again." He'd been hoping she'd ask him to anyway, but after this, he wasn't letting her out of his sight.

Daphne let out a sigh of relief and he knew in that moment he wouldn't attempt anything sexual tonight. She'd just had a scare and the last thing he ever wanted to do was take advantage of her. He just wanted to be there for her tonight. The need to protect and soothe her was almost overwhelming.

He righted the fallen bike and started it. He was thankful it didn't give him any problems, but he was definitely going to have it looked at. Luckily they only had a few blocks to go. "I'll drive."

When she didn't attempt to argue, he slid on the front and savored the feel of her wrapping herself around him. Yeah, if the vamp was behind this, that fucker was going to pay.

Chapter 8

"You weren't kidding about the crack of dawn." Daphne glanced at Hector as they strode up the walk toward her pack's mansion. The sun was just barely peeking over the horizon and it was colder than normal. The ride over had been nice since no one had been on the road, but her lungs burned from the chilly air.

"We're taking care of this now and this isn't the type of thing you tell your Alpha over the phone." There was no room for argument in his voice.

She was starting to learn that while Hector seemed incredibly laid-back, he had an underlying dominant streak. From the very limited experience she'd had with him in the bedroom, she had a feeling this was who he was at his core.

"You're so bossy," she muttered.

"You like it," he shot back.

She could feel her face heat up, but she didn't deny it. When he'd ordered her around in the bedroom it had been hot. And she wanted more of it.

During the day the pack left the front door unlocked—because seriously, who in their right mind would mess with lupine shifters—but at night they locked it. So she wasn't surprised that the door was locked now. She was shocked, however, when Hector pulled out a key. She had one too, but he wasn't pack. Apparently Angus *really* trusted him. That said a hell of a lot about his character because her Alpha kept his own pack on a short leash.

When they entered, the house was quiet. Her boots clicked against the marble floor, echoing in the foyer. She paused, worrying if they'd wake Angus and Iris.

Hector nodded toward the stairs. "I called him while you were in the shower."

Daphne's lips pulled into a thin line. "You could have told me."

"Sorry. I'm not used to... just sorry. I'm not trying to take over this situation. I want you safe and Angus needs to hear this from you."

"I know." She was dreading telling him, though.

When they reached Angus's office, which took forever to get to in the giant house, Daphne wiped sweaty palms on her jeans. She loved her Alpha. He was good and fair, but she'd never had much of a reason to see him for anything official. It was weird to be there now. Thankfully Hector was with her. He was such a calming influence without even trying. With his hand at the small of her back she was able to lose some of her nervousness.

Before she had a chance to knock, the door swung open. Angus stood on the other side, an easy smile on his face. He was tall, the same height as Hector, but much bigger. He reminded her of a pro-football player. Of course he was three hundred years old and a whole lot more badass. He looked to be in his forties, though, and was very handsome.

"Daphne. Hector." He nodded and noted the way Hector was holding her.

They'd shown up together at dawn so it was pretty obvious there was something going on between them, but she didn't like feeling as if she was under a microscope.

"Hi, Angus." She wiped her hands on her jeans again and her Alpha just shook his head.

He pulled her into a hug that immediately eased the rest of her lingering tension. "I can't believe you're nervous, child," he murmured.

She expelled a shaky laugh as she stepped back. "I feel like I'm being called into the principal's office or something."

"Sit and eat and we'll talk about what's going on." He motioned to an overstuffed couch by one of the big windows.

Her Alpha wasn't much on formality, but she was thankful to see he'd placed a tray of cookies and a coffee carafe on a bronze tray.

Hector took her hand and they both sat while Angus chose a seat across from them in a high-backed chair that reminded her of a throne. He sprawled out, looking at ease, but she knew a capable, brutal wolf lurked beneath the surface.

"Did you make this or did Iris?" she asked as Hector began to pour them two mugs, only half-joking.

Angus smiled suddenly, the action breaking up the harsh lines of his face. "God, I'd forgotten how cheeky you could be. You'll be happy to know my mate made the coffee and the cookies."

At hearing that, she snagged a cookie and practically inhaled it. She needed something since Hector had pretty much shoved her out the door that morning without sustenance. Once she'd eaten a few more, she jumped right in to what was going on with Troy, the human-turned-vampire. She'd even tried calling the new vampire the night before since she'd told him she would, but he hadn't answered. She couldn't shake the feeling that he was behind the SUV that had tried to ram them. She talked for a few minutes straight, barely taking a breath, and when she was done, she felt a million times lighter.

"And you haven't told your parents about this?" Angus asked after a long moment.

"No." She hadn't wanted to worry them.

"This isn't the pack way." There was a bite of censure in his words, but his dark eyes remained kind.

"I know and for that I'm sorry. Troy was a human and I just... I thought I could take care of this myself. It seemed so inconsequential and I didn't want to bother anyone with it."

"Nothing is inconsequential when it comes to the well-being of my people."

Okay, now she felt like a kid. And of course Hector was there to witness it. He'd been very quiet, letting her talk and not interrupting. He was definitely a rock, someone she could lean on. That thought scared the hell out of her because she was afraid to get used to it.

After a long moment, Angus gave a brief nod, almost to himself. Like he'd made a decision. "I'll take care of this. I think I might know who his maker is, and if not, I'll find out. You're going to let Hector shadow you until this is dealt with."

The thought of spending a lot of time with Hector was very appealing, but she didn't want him forced into it. That wasn't right and he could start to resent her. "Alpha, that's not necessary."

"You either accept this or move back to the mansion until this situation is settled." Angus's eyes went pure wolf for a moment, reminding her that he was her leader.

She looked at Hector, hoping to see if he was okay with this, but his expression was unreadable. Well, hell. She glanced back at Angus and nodded. "Hector can stay with me, but if it doesn't work out, I'll move back here." There, that would give him an out if he didn't want to spend all his free time with her. She couldn't get a read on him, and she was afraid that he might feel backed into a corner since Angus was practically ordering him.

Next to her, Hector growled low in his throat, but when she glanced at him, he was looking straight at Angus. "I need to talk to Angus alone, Daphne. I'll meet you downstairs in a few minutes," he said quietly.

Frowning, she looked back at her Alpha, who had a speculative gleam in his eyes. "If this is about the missing pregnant shifters, I want to hear what's going on. Leta's the one who called me and I have a right to know. A lot of my packmates are pregnant."

"Daphne, I need to talk to your Alpha in private." He wasn't being high-handed or rudely dismissing her, but she didn't like that there was no give in his voice, or that he wasn't offering her an explanation.

Gritting her teeth, she stood. "Fine." She'd find out more from her packmates later anyway. "Angus, thank you for dealing with Troy and if possible, maybe he doesn't have to get hurt?" She knew that would never be her decision now that her Alpha was involved but figured it didn't hurt to ask.

Angus grunted a non-response as his mouth lifted up at the corners—though it didn't look like a smile. More like he was trying not to bare his teeth. After a quick glance at Hector, who still wouldn't look at her, she exited the room. She knew that Angus's office was soundproofed for privacy and security reasons so she didn't bother trying to eavesdrop. Instead she headed downstairs and waited, even though she was seething inside at being left out by Hector of all people.

Chapter 9

Hector rubbed a hand over his face as he hurried down the stairs. He knew he'd annoyed Daphne, but he'd needed to talk to Angus and there was no way he'd planned to tell her what about. It wasn't as if he had to ask anyone for permission to mate with Daphne. That's not how things worked in the shifter world. But Angus was a good boss and he looked out for all supernatural beings in New Orleans, something he didn't have to do. Hector respected the man and he'd wanted to let him know what his intentions were.

And, if he was being honest, he wanted Angus to spread the word around to the Campbell pack that Daphne was off-limits. Angus hadn't been surprised and had even seemed happy about their possible mating.

Hector found Daphne outside on the front wraparound porch leaning against one of the pillars with her arms crossed over her chest. She pushed up and scowled when she saw him. "Done having your all-boys talk?" Sarcasm laced her words.

"I wasn't leaving you out to be rude or because I didn't think you shouldn't be privy to our conversation. What I needed to talk to Angus about was private. Not pack business and nothing to do with the missing shifters. Don't forget, he's my boss." Okay, their conversation had had nothing to do with work, but Hector didn't want to lie outright.

"Oh, right. Sorry." Her shoulders relaxed a fraction, but he could still see questions burning in her eyes.

He held up his bike keys. "I'll let you drive."

"You fight dirty."

"Hell, yeah." He tossed her the keys.

She caught them with a smile and turned away from him, sauntering down the drive with a not-quite-subtle sashay of her hips that drove him insane. He was sure she was intentionally teasing him and he didn't care. He loved watching her move like that.

The drive back to her place was slightly torturous considering how close he was pressed to Daphne and unable to do anything about it. But the second she turned his bike off, his entire body went on alert. That familiar scent of danger lingered in the air.

It wasn't something specific, but he'd sensed it the other night when Troy had shown up out of nowhere. The scent reminded him of darkness, like something greasy and oily lingering in the air.

"I smell it too," Daphne murmured and he looked down to find her gaze on him.

"We need to sweep your house." If that bastard Troy was in there, Hector was taking care of this right now.

"I'll go in from the back, you can take the front," Daphne said quietly.

If it was any other shifter, he'd say yes. But his jaguar wouldn't let her out of his sight. "We'll go in the front door together."

Her jaw tightened in annoyance, but she nodded. Slowly, they crept toward her townhouse. The scent faded the closer they got, but it still lingered in the air. Something else mixed in with the danger smell—blood. Coppery and distinctive.

Daphne shot him a hard look, telling him she smelled the same thing. As they neared the front door, he realized it was open a fraction. He couldn't smell any explosives residue or typical ingredients that went into bombs so he carefully toed the door open with his boot. He kept an arm out to shield Daphne, but she gasped at the same time he froze.

The mirror in her foyer had been smashed so that glass littered the tiled area, the foyer table was ripped apart, and there were smears of blood all over the wooden balustrade staircase. That was all Hector could see from their limited perspective and he wasn't about to let Daphne go in there. When she made a move to squeeze past him, he wrapped an arm around her waist and pulled her against his chest. "I'm calling Angus. Let him and whoever he brings deal with this. You don't need to see what was done to your house."

He thought she might argue, but she just turned and wrapped her arms around his waist. She buried her face against his chest and he hated the shiver that snaked through her. Someone had just trashed her home and he didn't even want to speculate where the blood had come from. If there was a body inside, Hector definitely didn't want Daphne seeing it. Not because he didn't think she could handle it, but why put her through it? Since he didn't hear a heartbeat inside, if there was someone in there they were dead. Whoever had done this had violated her belongings and her safe haven.

"Call him," she finally murmured. "If this was Troy, this has to stop."

Hector pulled out his cell with his free hand, tightening his grip around her as he slowly walked them away from the home. He didn't want her anywhere near the house until it was cleaned up. This was ending now, before Daphne was in any more danger.

Chapter 10

Five days later, Daphne was about to go crazy. Her boots clicked along the sidewalk as she strode with Saul toward the Full Moon. The city lights twinkled around them and the music and boisterous excitement from people out enjoying their lives was incredibly grounding. Hector needed to work and she wasn't about to monopolize all his time as her babysitter, but he'd asked her to come see him tonight and she wanted to get out of the mansion. Ever since her home had been trashed, there hadn't been a peep out of Troy—if he was even the person who'd done it. Deep down, she was pretty sure he was. He certainly wasn't returning her phone calls, which was pretty damning in her opinion.

And for the last five days she'd been cooped up in the pack's mansion. She and Hector had talked every day and he'd been by to see her a lot, but they hadn't had more than a moment of privacy. Plus she'd been attending school like normal—well, with an escort at all times. There was no way in hell she was going to let some psycho take that away from her. Now she was sexually frustrated beyond belief and had decided that tonight was it for her and Hector. She was pretty sure he felt the same way, though he was hard to read sometimes. He'd been really weird that morning when they'd talked on the phone, but she didn't know if that was about her or the whole situation and she hadn't wanted to analyze it.

"So what's the deal with you and Hector?" Saul asked.

Yeah, like she was going to tell him anything about her feelings for Hector. He was the biggest gossip of the pack. "We're friends."

Saul snorted. "Yeah, I make out with all my friends too."

"If you had any female friends, you probably would."

"You're my friend and I don't make out with you."

"But you would if I let you." Of that, she had no doubt. The man would hook up with anyone.

Grinning, Saul just shrugged in that charming manner of his. While she loved him and understood why females flocked to him, no one got her heart racing the way Hector did.

Music and laughter spilled from the bar as they approached. Saul went in ahead of her, as was male shifter custom—they had this thing for checking for possible danger—and stopped so suddenly she ran into his back.

He swiveled and looked down at her with pity. What the hell? He tried to stop her, but she peeked around him and saw some tall blonde female plastered against Hector, her mouth pressed against his. And Hector's hands were on her shoulders...

The sight was like a punch to her stomach. No, worse than that. Unwilling to watch the horrid display—or worse, start crying in front of half her pack—she turned on her heel and stalked down the sidewalk. If it had been any other time, she would have marched up to him and probably punched him in the face.

But the last week had left her raw and overly emotional and right now she didn't trust herself not to make a scene in front of shifters and humans alike. Some kid had developed a sick obsession with her and she was worried she'd somehow caused it. Add to that her growing feelings for Hector and—damn it, she was such an idiot. She refused to cry in front of anyone. It was the only reason she was hauling ass away from here.

Saul hurried beside her. "Daphne, he—"

She turned and shoved him in the chest, wishing it was Hector instead. She didn't want to hear some bullshit excuse from her own packmate. What was that anyway, some sort of male solidarity crap? Maybe she took Saul off guard because he stumbled back and sprawled on the sidewalk. He let out a yelp as his ass kissed the pavement.

Using those precious moments of freedom, she sprinted across the street and jumped into the back of an idling taxi that a man had been attempting to get into.

"Ma'am—"

Even though she knew it was an incredibly shitty thing to do, Daphne bared her canines. "Drive. I'll pay extra."

The guy's dark eyes widened and he jerked away from the curb. She heard someone shouting, probably his original patron, but she was beyond caring about anything at this point.

Her throat squeezed impossibly tight as she tried to hold back the sob building inside her. Part of her wished she'd been strong enough to confront Hector or yell at him... or something. But they'd never made any commitment to each other. They'd never even had sex. Sure, they'd made out a lot and he'd given her that one, intense orgasm, but they weren't a couple. No, screw him. This past week he'd made her feel as if she was the only female on the planet for him. As if what they had was special. Treating her like this was unforgivable.

"Where to, ma'am?" the driver asked, his voice wary.

She rattled off her address without thinking. Her pack had cleaned her place up and had a new alarm system installed, but she hadn't been back. She'd been too afraid, but right now she wasn't going to the mansion. She didn't want to see or talk to anyone. Nope, she wanted to be alone with her tears and she was pretty sure she had a bottle of wine in the pantry—if the bastard who'd trashed her place hadn't destroyed that too. Angus had refused to let her see inside her house until it was cleaned, but she'd heard some of her packmates whispering that someone had shredded her clothes and underwear. How gross was that?

When the driver pulled up to her place she shoved a wad of cash at him and apologized for being so rude. She hoped the giant tip made up for it, but she didn't have the energy to say much more.

Tears tracked down her face, nearly blinding her as she hurried toward her front door. She froze at the sound of a bullet being chambered. While she might not use weapons, almost every shifter had knowledge of guns and knives. And she knew that sound. Standing on the bottom stair that led to her front door, she slowly turned around and tried to ignore the icy chill slithering through her veins.

Troy was standing there and he had a gun pointed right at her face.

Chapter 11

Hector felt like he was going to vomit right on the floor of the bar. He wiped his mouth, as if that could somehow erase the feel and taste of that drunk human's lips on his. He'd cut her off earlier, but she must have been sneaking drinks, so when he'd tried to kick her out, she'd literally thrown herself at him.

If she'd been a shifter, he'd have thrown her ass across the bar, but she was human and they were so damn fragile. He'd still shoved her off of him, but not soon enough. Hector had heard of the effects of the mating call, but this was beyond what he'd expected. He actually felt physically ill after being fondled by the woman.

Jax, one of the female bouncers, gripped the human female's arm, mainly to keep her standing upright. "I'm going to get her into a cab."

"She's banned for life," Hector growled. "I've already got a copy of her ID."

"Hector, that's kinda harsh," Jax said almost admonishingly.

"What would you do if someone kissed and groped you against your will?" None of the females in the bar would put up with that shit. He wouldn't either. "I'm not Saul," he added as an afterthought, because that male probably would have liked it.

Jax nodded once in approval. "If someone did that to me they wouldn't be walking for a week." She propelled the woman toward the door. "Did you hear that, honey? Banned for life."

He scrubbed a hand over his face in time to see Saul striding through the bar looking pissed. Hector's eyes widened when he realized the lupine shifter was stalking toward him like he was prey.

Barely dodging the other shifter's fist when he took a swing, Hector ducked down and put some distance between them. The music quieted and the dance floor cleared as Saul turned to face him.

"What the hell, Saul?"

The lupine shifter's hands were balled into fists and his wolf was crystal clear in his gaze. "You can't treat Daphne like that."

He frowned. "What are you talking about?"

"She saw you kissing that woman and she deserves better than that." Saul growled deep in his throat, the first time Hector had ever seen him truly pissed about anything. Normally he was all about having a good time and chasing after females.

Fuck. "That female kissed me and she's now banned for life. I didn't want that shit and... I don't need to explain myself to you. Where the hell is Daphne?"

Some of the tension fled Saul's body as he shrugged. "She ran off and got into a cab."

Hector's heart beat wildly in his chest. Daphne was out there alone? There was still a threat against her. Angus had tracked down

Troy's maker—a young punk who had no business turning unstable humans into vamps—but they hadn't been able to find Troy. The guy had gone underground, but it was only a matter of time before he came after Daphne again.

Hector pulled out his phone and dialed her cell. It went to voice mail after a couple rings, meaning she'd likely ignored the call. Cursing, he looked at Saul who was still watching him warily. "You're taking my shift tonight. I'm going to find Daphne. And for the record, I would never hurt her. I'm going to mate her if she'll have me." He said it loud enough for the entire bar to hear before he raced outside.

Right now he didn't give a shit about anyone but Daphne. If she actually thought he'd cheated on her... His inner jaguar clawed at his insides, telling him to make this right. He should have made his intentions clear earlier, but she'd had so much shit piled on her plate and they'd had literally no privacy. But mainly, his feelings for her were damn powerful and almost overwhelming. He didn't want to scare her into running from him.

As he jogged toward his bike, he tried calling her again multiple times, but it kept going to voicemail. Jumping on his bike, he tried to think of where she'd go. The mansion was a no-go. She was likely pissed and hurt right now. She wouldn't want to be surrounded by her packmates. And she wouldn't go to Leta's because that was his sister. Gunning the engine, he tore out into traffic. It could be the wrong guess, but he had to start somewhere. She hadn't been back to her place since it had been cleaned up.

He had to find her. To make this right. He refused to let a misunderstanding rip them apart. His jaguar was snarling and urging him to go faster. Breaking a dozen traffic laws, he made it to her street in less than five minutes. As his bike roared up to her place, he lost a decade of his life as he saw the vamp Troy pointing a gun at Daphne.

No doubt it had silver bullets. If she'd been a little older, she might survive a direct shot to the head. But she was still growing in strength and if the silver got in her bloodstream—his jaguar clawed, taking over before Hector could think about maintaining control.

His bones broke, ligaments snapped and everything realigned as fur replaced skin in milliseconds. He'd never shifted that fast. He'd also never cared about anyone the way he did about Daphne. For years he'd locked down that spark of the mating call he'd felt when she'd been nineteen. He'd convinced himself the reaction to her couldn't have been as intense as he'd remembered. But he hadn't been able to swallow his own lies to himself. Kinda hard to when he hadn't been able to touch another female since their almost kiss so many years ago.

The vamp turned at the sound of his snarled cry, moving the gun away from Daphne's body. Hector saw her duck and kick out at the vamp, slamming her boot into his stomach with a vicious blow.

Everything happened in slow motion. Troy stumbled back, his gun-toting hand wavering about wildly. Daphne made a move to attack the vamp again, but Hector was faster.

And this kill was his. Using all the strength in his hind legs, he launched himself through the air. His paws slammed into Troy's chest. The gun flew out of the vamp's hand and his claws came out. Vamp claws were sharp and just as deadly as shifters'. The vamp clawed at Hector's face and tried to dig into his side, but Hector was ending this before it started.

He wouldn't be much of a fighter if he couldn't take this punk out. His inner jaguar wanted to torment and play with the prey for daring to hurt Daphne, but he reined in those instincts and snapped his jaw around Troy's neck.

Crunching through bone and ligaments, he tasted sweet vamp blood as Troy's body went completely limp beneath him. Tearing and pulling, Hector finally yanked the head from his body, tossing it a few feet away. With his adrenaline pumping, he hovered over the carnage and tried to get himself under control.

The need to hunt and kill was always strong in him—he was a natural born predator—but he'd never been out of control before. Not like this. For the first time in his life the pull of the animal was stronger than the man.

"Hector?"

He turned at the sound of Daphne's soft voice. She stood a few feet away, but she didn't look afraid of him. Thank God for that.

"Can you come back to me? He's dead. He won't hurt me anymore." Her voice shook a little, but her relief was palpable.

Hearing those words was all he needed. In the distance he heard sirens blaring and had no doubt they were meant for him. A neighbor would have definitely called the cops by now. Before shit went crazy and they had to explain to the humans what was going on, he needed to clear one thing up with the woman he loved.

Shifting back to human form was a little quicker and seconds later he was standing in front of Daphne naked and completely unselfconscious. He wanted to reach out and comfort her, but wasn't sure she'd welcome it. "Did he hurt you?"

She shook her head and he saw anger, not sadness, in her gaze. "No. He was planning to, though."

He would ask more later, but he'd needed that out of the way first. "I didn't kiss that woman at the bar. She kissed me, taking me completely by surprise. It was fucking disgusting. I don't want to touch or kiss anyone but you, Daphne. I love you. I realized it—"

Before he could finish she launched herself at him. He was covered in blood, but she wrapped her arms and legs around him and almost tackled him to the ground with the intensity of her kiss.

Behind him, he heard tires screeching and doors slamming. It was the only thing that made them pull apart from one another.

"Hands in the air!" a man shouted.

Taking a deep breath, he set Daphne on her feet and they both raised their arms. Until the cops figured out what was going on, this was going to be a huge hassle.

But once it was settled, he was going to complete this conversation with Daphne, then finish what he'd started the night he'd first kissed her.

Chapter 12

Daphne sat on the back of the ambulance between the open doors. The human paramedics were nice and had given her a blanket to wrap around herself even though she hadn't needed it. But it seemed to make them feel better so she kept it and accepted the hot tea one of the females had given her. Once everything had been ironed out with the police she and Hector had been treated like victims, not criminals. Well, for the most part. Hector had just killed a vampire, but luckily humans didn't worry much about violence between paranormal beings. If Troy had been a human, however, things would have ended much differently.

She was pretty sure the way the cops had eased up had everything to do with a handsome detective, Colt McCarty, who was friends with Angus. Detective McCarty was now talking to Hector two police car lengths away, but Daphne could hear everything.

Not that it mattered. The detective was just repeating the same thing Hector had told them an hour ago, but actually putting it all on paper now for an official statement.

She couldn't believe Troy was dead, but he'd pointed a gun at her head. Most of her sympathy for the guy had disappeared in that instant. Messed-up childhood or not, he would have only grown more dangerous the older and more powerful he became if he'd been allowed to live as a vampire. Shuddering at the thought, she tightened the blanket around her, actually grateful for it now.

As she sat there, Angus arrived with Iris. They hurried from their truck at the same time and walked in perfect unison together. Both were tall and moved with a liquid grace, though Iris was curvier, very feminine, and had perfect bronze-hued skin thanks to her Greek heritage. Right now she looked worried and the concern on her face had nothing to do with what had happened tonight. Daphne wasn't sure how she knew it, but she did.

The cops didn't even attempt to stop them, just lifted the yellow crime scene tape and let them under. Yeah, they were well known in New Orleans.

Tossing off the blanket, she stood and met them halfway, stopping in front of one of the oaks that lined her street. "What is it?"

"How are you holding up?" Angus asked quietly.

"Fine. Why are you here? This isn't about me, is it? Is it Leta?" Out of the corner of her eye, she saw Hector tense, his head whip in their direction.

Iris shook her head sharply. "Not Leta, but another feline has gone missing. Hector's sister called Angus in a panic when she couldn't get a hold of either of you."

"Crap," Daphne muttered. She'd turned her phone off because she hadn't wanted to deal with her parents or concerned packmates, and Hector had probably lost his sometime during his shift. At least one of the cops had found him some pants and a T-shirt to wear. "Do they know if she was taken for sure?"

Angus nodded, but he didn't offer any more explanation and she didn't push. The details weren't important at the moment. Making sure it didn't happen again and getting these women back safely was what mattered. "Is Leta safe?"

"I have some of the pack watching her house. They're taking shifts," Angus said.

"Thank you. I appreciate you looking out for her, and I mean this with all the respect in the world, but this won't solve the problem. What the hell is going on in our city? Why would anyone want to kidnap pregnant shifters?"

Angus's jaw clenched tightly, but his anger wasn't directed at her. "The police and our pack are working on it, but I've called the Council. They're sending someone as soon as they can. And I have no idea why anyone would do something like this."

She almost snorted at the mention of the Council. They were no better than shifty politicians, but if they sent the enforcer to help, that might actually make a difference. There was no way her best friend could be kept under lock and key her entire pregnancy. Not only that, but there were tons of other pregnant shifters in the city. Someone had to look out for the well-being of all of them.

Hector walked up at that moment and wrapped his arm around Daphne's shoulders. "They're letting us leave," he said to Angus, who simply nodded. Then he looked down at her. "I heard what you guys were talking about. I'd like to see Leta tonight if you're up to it."

Like he even had to ask. She leaned up and kissed his cheek, not caring that they had an audience. She knew he was okay physically, but she was still a little shaken up about what he'd done. "I'm ready to go when you are."

Since Hector's bike was scratched and dented to hell, they said their good-byes to Angus and Iris then took Daphne's car. The ride was short, but neither of them said much on the way over. Daphne was still reeling from when he'd told her that he loved her. She loved him too but didn't want to tell him right before they pulled up to his sister's house. No, she wanted to tell him and then spend hours showing him exactly how she felt.

Chapter 13

Daphne knew she should be wiped out after the insane night she and Hector had just had. But as Hector opened the door to his two-bedroom cottage style bungalow in Uptown, the only thing she wanted to do was get him naked. She didn't have as much experience as he likely did, but she was a shifter and sensual by nature.

He tossed his keys onto an antique looking table by the front door as he closed and locked it. His place was masculine, with lots of browns, greens and tans and all antique furniture. The art on the walls had likely been bought from street artists in the Square. Paintings of saxophone players, fleur-de-lis and a gorgeous oil painting of Chartres Street in the rain revealed his attachment to the city. "Do we still need to talk about what happened at the bar?"

He'd been very physically affectionate at Leta's house, pulling Daphne into his lap on the couch while they talked and calmed his sister down. But they hadn't talked about what she'd seen and why she'd run from him. "Not unless you were lying." She knew he hadn't been and when he growled softly, she didn't hide her smile.

"Then why'd you run? Why didn't you stay and confront me? And how could you *ever* think I'd cheat on you?" He looked and sounded hurt.

She hated the way she'd reacted. "After the past couple weeks, hell, months at school having to dodge that lunatic, I was feeling raw and unsure about *everything*. Then this past week we didn't have any private time and I thought... I guess I thought maybe I'd read into stuff or you'd changed your mind or... I don't know. I was being stupid and emotional. I did think about punching you, though. Right before I almost burst into tears."

"Saul tried to," Hector said wryly.

Daphne's eyes widened. "I'm sorry I didn't have more faith in you."

"In *us*. I want to mate with you, Daphne. More than I've ever wanted anything. I've been trying to take things slowly because I didn't want to scare you with the intensity of how I feel."

"Scare me?" Not possible. She'd wanted him for too long. And she knew he wanted her now. Well, more than just that. Still... "Can I ask you something?" When he nodded she continued. "Remember what happened right before I went to college... why did you stop me from kissing you? Were you not attracted to me then?" She could feel her face heat up as she asked. She hadn't changed that much since then and while it had been years ago, she'd never forget how embarrassed she'd felt afterward. Putting miles between them had been the best thing. Even then she hadn't been able to move on, settle for someone else. She simply hadn't been able to do it.

He looked surprised by her question. Then he paused so long she wondered if he wouldn't answer. Finally he spoke. "I was *very* attracted to you, but you were buzzing from too many drinks and I didn't trust myself to stop at just kissing. And you deserved better than that, especially since you were leaving. You needed to get away from your pack and figure out who you were. If we'd started something, you would have ended up staying here."

When she started to respond, he shook his head. "I know myself and I wouldn't have wanted to let you go. His eyes went pure jaguar for a moment then flashed back to startling green. "I can be territorial and possessive and I hate when other males look at you. When Neil asked you out during our dinner, it took all my control not to pummel that little shit. If we mate, I know a lot of that will fade since we'll be scented with each other, but I'm still territorial as hell where you're concerned. I... haven't been with anyone since you left. It's like my jaguar was sleeping until you came back."

Her mouth parted slightly at his confession, his words sending a ribbon of awareness and pleasure spiraling through her. What he'd just admitted was huge and she wanted to savor it. The peace she felt at his words was something her wolf side needed to hear too, to know how much she meant to him. Because she'd never been with anyone—and wanted him to be her first and only lover.

And she liked that he was territorial. Mated shifters were notoriously possessive of each other and over the past week he'd been so casual about everything. Laid-back, the Hector she thought she knew. She was glad she brought out this side of him. It was the way things were supposed to be with mates. "I feel the same way and you know I love you too . . . right?" She hadn't said the words, mainly because saying them aloud scared her a little. She was afraid that if she did, she'd wake up and discover everything between them was all a dream.

He pushed out a harsh breath. "I needed to hear the words."

She loved the relief she heard in his voice, loved knowing he was just as torn up over her as she was over him. Right now, she didn't want any more words. They loved each other and they wanted to mate. That was all she needed to know. Grasping the hem of her sweater, she tugged it over her head. His place was slightly heated, but the cool air rushed over her body, chilling her.

Hector sucked in sharply as his gaze raked over her. "Take off your boots and pants." A soft order.

She did as he said, slowly peeling the rest of her clothes off. When she was fully naked, he pressed his body up against hers, walking them backward until her spine flattened against the wall in the front hallway. Then he surprised the hell out of her by kneeling at her feet. She was tall, but so was he and his head was a little above her mound.

"Put one foot over my shoulder," he growled softly.

Her entire body tightened at the demand. She did as he said, opening herself up to him. The position made her feel exposed, but not vulnerable. Hector would never hurt her. Since he'd killed Troy she realized that he only wanted to protect and take care of her. She felt the same about him.

He inhaled, breathing in her scent, and she squirmed under his intense scrutiny. Before she had a chance to even think about being self-conscious, his mouth was on her, teasing and licking.

The feel of his mouth and tongue stroking her sent her senses into overdrive. Clutching his head with both hands, she moved her raised leg up so that her foot was on his shoulder, not slung over it. As a shifter she was flexible and this position gave him better access and her more pleasure.

Going deeper than he had before, he slid his tongue into her, tasting her wet heat. He might be on his knees but he was the one in control right now. With each of his teasing strokes, her hips rolled against his face. She threaded her fingers through his dark hair and let go of all sense of control. She was barely hanging onto it anyway.

Letting go was freeing, and though she shouldn't have been surprised, the sharp climax that rushed through her took her off guard. Using just his tongue, he increased pressure on her clit. Removing her hands from his head, she slammed her palms against the wall so she wouldn't accidentally claw him. Her sensitive bundle of nerves felt so damn raw, but he just kept stroking and extending her orgasm until her knees weakened and buckled under her.

But he was faster than her. Scooping her up, he strode down a hallway, nuzzling her neck as he walked. She wrapped her arms around his neck, breathing in his spicy scent. Her surroundings were a blur, but she was aware of when they stepped into his bedroom because his masculine scent grew stronger. As he pulled her earlobe between his teeth, murmuring something about her being beautiful, she was vaguely aware of the massive bed, but he bypassed it and nudged open another door into a dimly lit bathroom.

For a brief moment she wondered what he was doing, but quickly realized his intent. The cops had given him some towels to clean up with but he'd want to shower before they made love.

Daphne's experience with males was limited, but with him everything was instinctual. Shifters weren't built like humans and her first time wouldn't be painful. Maybe uncomfortable but that was it.

Instead of waiting for him to undress, she grasped his shirt and practically yanked it over his head. Her hands shook as he was bared to her. There were still traces of blood on his chest and that angered her inner wolf, but when his hand cupped her cheek and he gently rubbed her bottom lip with his thumb, most of that dissipated.

"It's just you and me right now. No one's going to hurt us," he said quietly, as if he'd read her mind.

Hell, he'd probably read her emotions. Around him she didn't hide them very well. She wanted to take off the rest of his clothes, but he was lightning fast, almost ripping the cargo pants to get them off. Then he was standing in front of her in a way she'd only fantasized about and *oh my* . . . Her gaze landed on his hard length and she swallowed hard. What she'd felt multiple times through his pants definitely lived up to the hype she'd created in her head. More so.

Involuntarily she clenched her legs together and he just grinned before pulling her to him. His erection lay hot and hard against her belly. "Shower with me?"

She nodded.

He cleared his throat and a trickle of nervousness rolled off him. The acidic scent surprised her. There was nothing this man had to be nervous about. Lord, had he ever looked in the mirror?

"Mate with me now?" he asked and that acidic scent intensified.

She linked her fingers behind his neck and looked up at him, surprised at the uncertainty lurking in his green eyes. She'd thought that was exactly what they'd been planning to do. Clearly he hadn't realized she'd wanted it this instant. After his confession that he hadn't been with anyone since she'd been away at college, she knew without a doubt—even without her wolf side accepting him fully—that this was the male for her. For always. "I don't want to wait. I want you forever, Hector. There's never been anyone else for me. Just you." She also wanted to bond, but knew that was something they'd talk about in the future.

"There's not a full moon right now, but... I want to bond with you too." His words stole her breath. It was as if he'd read her mind. "You don't have to make a decision now. I just want to lay everything out there. I'm not letting you go."

"Try and get rid of me." She knew she probably looked goofy with the giant grin plastered on her face, but knowing he wanted to bond too filled her with awe. It was the ultimate sign of love for shifters. Unlike mated shifters, who could eventually walk away if they chose, much in the way humans divorced each other, bonded mates were separated only in death. And couples could become bondmates only during a full moon when the male took the female from behind, sinking his canines into her neck, marking her.

"So that's a yes?"

Growling softly, she nipped his bottom lip with her teeth. "Like you even have to ask?"

With that, his mouth was on hers, hungry and needy. One second they were standing in the middle of the bathroom, the next they were in his giant granite and glass shower enclosure.

Hot water rushed around them as she wrapped her legs around his waist. Her inner walls were desperate to be filled by him but she didn't want to tear her lips from his. Never wanted to stop kissing him.

After what felt like an eternity he drew his head back, his breathing ragged, his eyes bright with hunger. Water rolled down his face and chest as he rubbed a hand over his damp hair. "I need you now." The words were ragged and unsteady.

Just how she felt inside. Without another word, she turned and placed her hands on the slick, cool tiled wall. Everything about this moment with him was erotic and sensual. Her entire body was shaking as his big hands curved around her hips.

He flexed his fingers as he slid a knee between her legs. Spreading them farther apart, she tried to grasp the wall but there was no give.

One of his hands slid up her waist and cupped her breast, strumming her already hard nipple as he pushed his hard length into her. The intrusion was welcome but still a shock to her senses. Her inner walls stretched to mold around him and he paused, letting her adjust. Little tremors erupted throughout her body as he pushed all the way inside her. She couldn't believe it, but she was ready to come again.

All he'd have to do was move a few times. She was already trembling with the need to climax for a second time.

Still buried deep inside her, he leaned down and she felt the sharp tips of his canines raking against her neck. He didn't puncture the skin, just grazed it. As he did, he pulled almost all the way out of her, then thrust back in.

She moaned as he started moving inside her in a steady, yet barely controlled rhythm. He filled her in a way she hadn't known was possible. She could feel his need and energy pulsing off him in waves, but he was holding back until she came again. When he pressed his canines against her neck, she lost it.

The orgasm that ripped through her this time was nothing compared to the others he'd given her. She let out a primal shout, not caring how out of control she sounded as she came.

It was then that he pierced her skin. For a brief moment it stung, but that quickly gave way to pleasure and when she felt his own climax, she pushed harder against him as he thrust into her.

He growled her name as she wrung the last vestiges of his orgasm from him before wrapping his arms around her and tugging her against his chest. Still half-hard inside her, he gently nuzzled her neck where he'd marked her.

Satisfaction spread through her. Now all supernatural beings would know they were taken because of their scents. And when they bonded, he'd receive a tattooed mark somewhere on his body, proclaiming to the whole damn world that he was hers. She couldn't wait.

"I love you so much," she whispered. Even with the water rushing over them, her words seemed to echo.

"I love you too." His words were harsher than hers and when he turned her around, the love she saw shining in his eyes floored her. Most of all, it thrilled her.

He kissed her, his strokes teasing yet still hungry and when she felt his insistent erection against her stomach, she realized they were just getting started for the night. That was fine with her. There was nothing she'd rather do than spend the night loving her mate.

Epilogue

Three days later

Daphne opened the door to her and Hector's home and hung up her keys on the hooks she'd put up. Since his place hadn't been tainted with any craziness from Troy she'd decided she'd rather move in with Hector than the other way around. Plus now she was a lot closer to school.

Saul and a few packmates had decided to move into her previous home and she could only imagine that they'd already turned it into a horrible bachelor pad.

Exhausted from a full day of classes, she headed into the kitchen, ready to open a bottle of red wine, but froze when she saw Hector sitting at the table with his head in his hands. She'd known he was home but now that she was in the kitchen a sour, lemony scent assaulted her at once. Grief.

"Oh, shit," she muttered before she could stop herself.

He looked up, his face etched with pain. "Leta's been taken," he said, his voice broken as he looked up at her.

The words echoed hollowly inside her. Daphne dropped her purse and covered the distance between them in seconds. Tears were already falling down her cheeks as she wrapped her arms around Hector. He buried his face in her neck and she felt his own tears on her skin. "What happened?" she asked hoarsely. She'd just talked to her friend that morning and everything had been fine.

Hector pulled his head back but tugged her into his lap. "She and Cesar were out to lunch. She went to the bathroom in a *public* fucking place and"—his voice broke but after a few moments he wrestled his control back and continued—"she never came back. It's not just her, though. Imelda from your pack was also taken. Your entire pack is going insane right now."

Daphne tried to digest all his words. She'd turned her phone to silent while she'd been in school all day so she could only imagine she had dozens of missed calls. *Shit, shit, shit.* More tears fell freely. Leta was truly missing. How could that be? Her mate, Cesar, had to be tearing himself up right now. They needed to be with him. "What did Angus say?"

"We're going out on a search party in half an hour. He's getting everyone together, but…" He shook his head, his normally bright eyes dull and filled with agony.

He didn't need to finish. New Orleans and the surrounding areas were massive. If someone was taking pregnant shifters there were so many places to hide them and clearly whoever was behind these kidnappings wasn't afraid of the Campbell pack. They'd been targeting felines up until now, but today they'd taken not only a feline, but a *lupine*. And Imelda was incredibly loved by the pack. That was a ballsy move. "We're going to find her and everyone else." They had to. Daphne refused to believe they were dead either.

Hector ran a hand over his face. "Angus said the newest enforcer is on the way. She should be here tomorrow."

She? Daphne had heard rumors of a new enforcer appointed by the Council, but she'd wondered if it had been bullshit. Now she was incredibly grateful for an enforcer's presence. They lived by their own set of rules, and as far as she knew, an enforcer had never failed a job. Maybe those were bullshit rumors too, but right now she'd hold on to that hope.

"We're going to find her," she repeated again, stronger this time, needing to say the words for Hector as much as for herself.

He tightened his grip around her for a long moment, then stood, a mask of anger and determination covering his face. The rage pulsing from him chilled her. "You're right. We will. And when we find out who's behind this, they're going to die."

Dear Readers

Thank you for reading the latest Moon Shifter story! If you'd like to stay in touch and be the first to learn about new releases you can:

Check out my website for book news: https://www.katiereus.com

Also, please consider leaving a review at one of your favorite online retailers. It's a great way to help other readers discover new books and I appreciate all reviews.

Happy reading,
Katie

Moon Shifter Sneak Peeks

Primal Possession © 2012

December McIntyre managed to smile at her date as he pulled out her chair for her. Her cheeks hurt from all the fake smiles and forced laughter. She should never have agreed to this date when she'd rather be anywhere else.

With *someone* else.

But she and Liam had no future, and going out with a random guy was the only way to show Liam *and* herself that she was serious about that.

"Have you been here before?" her date—Mike something—asked. As a tourist from the nearby ski lodge, he wasn't a local of her smaller mountain community, so it made sense he'd never eaten at the cozy Italian restaurant.

She nodded. "The *bucatini puttanesca* is really good. So is the *pollo caprese*. Actually, everything on the menu is good." The Russo family had settled in Fontana, North Carolina, decades ago, many years before she'd been born, and Russo Ristorante had become a staple in the mountain community. The locals loved it and so did the tourists. Occasionally they even got tourists from not just Fontana Mountain but their neighbors, Beech and Sugar mountains.

Almost immediately after they ordered drinks, her date excused himself. He was a broker or something and had to take an important call—apparently this late in the evening. Normally that would have bothered her in a date, but she didn't really care about this one. She wanted to get through the meal, get home, and just go to bed. She'd known agreeing to the date was a mistake the second after she'd said yes.

Because all she could think about was Liam. Liam with his broad shoulders, dark hair, and coffee brown, deep knowing eyes. When that man looked at her, she got shivers. The good kind. He didn't have to do *anything* other than train that heated gaze on her and she wanted to melt into his arms. He might be built like a linebacker, but his hands were sweet and gentle. At least the few times he'd caressed her face, they had been.

Her image of him was so clear she could almost see him now. In front of her. Wait... she blinked. He *was* in front of her, walking straight toward her.

"Crap," she muttered. Tensing, she braced herself. She'd thought if he saw her leaving her bookstore—because she'd seen him watching—with another guy on a Friday night, he'd get the hint and leave her alone. If it was anyone else, she might think he was acting like a creepy stalker, but she knew him better than that. As one of the few lupine shifters who lived in their town, Liam had tried to warn her about some crazy fanatic group that wanted to hurt humans involved with shifters. He was worried they wanted to hurt her, but she wasn't involved with a shifter so there was no *reason* for some fanatics to come after her. And at twenty-eight years old, she'd been taking care of herself for a long time.

Should have known Liam wouldn't give up so easily. The maître d' led him and another huge guy directly to the table next to hers. There was a decent amount of space between them, but for the way he was watching her, he might as well have been sitting at the same table.

"Hello, December." Liam's deep, intoxicating voice forced her to acknowledge him.

She flicked a quick look at his dark-haired friend, who cracked a small, almost amused smile until she glared at him—then she focused on Liam. "What are you doing here?" she asked through gritted teeth.

He shrugged as if it should be obvious. "Eating."

"You know what I mean. I'm on a *date*, Liam."

At the word "date" those dark eyes of his got even darker. Under normal circumstances she might have thought it was the light playing tricks on her, but she knew better. She'd seen him enraged once before when a man had tried to mug her. His eyes had changed then. The whites had almost disappeared and she'd found herself staring into not-quite-human eyes. He'd later explained that it sometimes happened when his inner wolf wanted to take over.

It had scared her then but not now. She knew he wouldn't hurt her, not physically. He might be dominating and sometimes too pushy, but he cared for her. In another world she might allow herself to care for him too. But they had no chance and she wasn't going to risk getting her heart broken and losing her only family due to involvement with Liam. Especially when anything that happened between them couldn't last. He barely looked thirty, but she knew he was over a hundred years old.

"Get rid of him." He didn't raise his voice, but there was a razor-sharp edge to it.

"Or what?"

"Or I'll do it for you."

"So how far from your place are we?" Self-loathing bubbled up inside her as she asked the question.

Scott's dark eyes glanced her way and he grinned before turning his gaze back to the road in front of him. "Not far, baby. Not far."

Baby? How about, *barf.* Before she could dwell on it she sniffed the air. Something sensual rolled off him and it took her a moment to realize it was lust. She was still getting used to tapping into her extrasensory abilities and deciphering one smell from another. This was like a sweet wine, clean and refreshing.

It reminded her that even though she might not care about this guy or plan to see him again, he didn't seem like a bad person with bad intentions. It was the reason she'd chosen him tonight. Before she'd been turned into a shifter she'd been a human but also a seer. Just like her mom. Back then she'd only been able to see the true faces of supernatural beings.

She'd been able to see the wolves or jaguars or whatever kind of animal lurked beneath the surface of shifters. And with vamps, she'd been able to see their teeth and their hunger for blood. After being turned into a shifter she could also see the truth of humans' nature. It was a weird addition to her psychic abilities. With the ability to see the truth about people, she could see Scott's "real" face. He was just a horny guy looking to get laid. No darker intentions or freaky sexual proclivities.

As they pulled into the driveway of a cottage-style house in a normal-looking middle-class neighborhood, she took another deep breath. She could do this. Couldn't she?

When he put the truck in park, she fought the growing dread inside her and dragged in a breath. With a numb hand she opened the door and slid out of the vehicle. The second her boots hit the pavement of the driveway she knew she couldn't go through with this. Not if she wanted to look at herself in the mirror the next morning.

One-night stands weren't her style, and while she desperately needed control in her life, the thought of this guy's hands on her body made her nauseous. Not because he was bad-looking or gave her bad vibes, but because she didn't want this from a stranger. Not truly. As she started to walk around the truck to Scott's side, she turned at the sound of a motorcycle pulling into the driveway behind them.

What. The. Hell.

Jayce. Fury punched through her as she watched him ride up. Well, fury and something else that she refused to define. It might have been relief, but she wasn't going to go there. Not tonight.

Not when anger was so much easier.

Stalking toward Jayce as he slid off the bike, she tried to keep her gaze from trailing down to those incredibly muscular legs. Didn't matter that he was wearing jeans. She'd seen every inch of his naked body and the image was seared into her brain. He moved with such fluidity, such power—it had always amazed her.

Even now, when she wanted to pummel him for having the audacity to follow her, she still had to admire the strength and power he radiated. He would never be called handsome, or even good-looking, but there was something dangerous about Jayce that was incredibly sexy. Without even trying, he exuded a raw sexuality that made women stand up and take notice. With his shaved head and a scar that crisscrossed over his left eye, he had a presence that refused to be ignored and the scar only added to that edginess. And he was directing all of that at her with a *very* heated stare.

"What the hell are you doing here?" she growled.

Before he could answer, Scott was next to her, in front of her actually, partially blocking her from Jayce. "Can I help you, buddy?"

Kat smiled haughtily at Jayce. At least Scott wasn't a total wimp.

But then Jayce trained his gaze on the other man. Jayce was scary when he wanted to be, and as she watched his normally gunmetal gray eyes turn to black, she actually had to force herself to stand her ground. He growled low in his throat. "You can go inside your fucking house and leave us alone."

Scott cleared his throat nervously, then looked at her. "You, uh, know this guy?"

Bitter and acidic, she could smell the fear on him. So much for not being a wimp. Ignoring Scott, she turned back to Jayce and set her hands on her hips. "Did you *follow* me here?"

"What do you think?" he practically purred as he took a step closer.

Now she scented something dark and rich, like chocolate. *Lust.* As a human she'd never had a clue that lust or desire actually had a smell, but now... oh, this was addicting. She inhaled and for a moment she felt light-headed. But when she saw the knowing look in Jayce's eyes, she snapped. "I think it's pathetic that you're following me around like a little puppy dog." She knew he still wanted her and the knowledge made her feel powerful. Even if she was playing with fire by taunting him, it gave her perverse pleasure to see the anger flare in that newly darkened gaze.

"Puppy dog?" His voice was low, a soft, menacing growl that made the hair on her arms stand straight up.

Next to her Scott actually took a step back, using her body to block his own. "Should I, uh, call the cops?" he squeaked out.

"No. Just go inside and forget you met me." She didn't look at him and he didn't question her directive. She heard him shuffle away, then fumble for his keys. They hit the pavement once, then seconds later she heard the front door slamming closed.

Jayce continued to stare at her, his chest falling and rising erratically. Oh, yeah, she'd pissed him off really good. And she really, really loved that. God, she was so messed up right now.

"Get. On. My. Bike."

About the Author

Katie Reus is the *USA Today* bestselling author of the Red Stone Security series, the Ancients Rising series and the Redemption Harbor series. She fell in love with romance at a young age thanks to books she pilfered from her mom's stash. Years later she loves reading romance almost as much as she loves writing it.

However, she didn't always know she wanted to be a writer. After changing majors many times, she finally graduated summa cum laude with a degree in psychology. Not long after that she discovered a new love. Writing. She now spends her days writing paranormal romance and sexy romantic suspense. If you would like to be notified of future releases, please visit her website: https://katiereus.com and join her newsletter.

Complete Booklist

Ancients Rising

Ancient Protector

Ancient Enemy

Ancient Enforcer

Ancient Vendetta

Ancient Retribution

Ancient Vengeance

Ancient Sentinel

Ancient Warrior

Ancient Guardian

Darkness Series

Darkness Awakened

Taste of Darkness

Beyond the Darkness

Hunted by Darkness

Into the Darkness

Saved by Darkness

Guardian of Darkness

Sentinel of Darkness

A Very Dragon Christmas

Darkness Rising

Deadly Ops Series

Targeted

Bound to Danger

Chasing Danger

Shattered Duty

Edge of Danger

A Covert Affair

Endgame Trilogy

Bishop's Knight

Bishop's Queen

Bishop's Endgame

Holiday With a Hitman Series

How the Hitman Stole Christmas

MacArthur Family Series

Falling for Irish

Unintended Target

Saving Sienna

Moon Shifter Series

Alpha Instinct

Lover's Instinct

Primal Possession

Mating Instinct

His Untamed Desire

Avenger's Heat

Hunter Reborn

Protective Instinct

Dark Protector

A Mate for Christmas

O'Connor Family Series

Merry Christmas, Baby

Tease Me, Baby

It's Me Again, Baby

Mistletoe Me, Baby

Red Stone Security Series®

No One to Trust

Danger Next Door

Fatal Deception

Miami, Mistletoe & Murder

His to Protect

Breaking Her Rules

Protecting His Witness

Sinful Seduction
Under His Protection
Deadly Fallout
Sworn to Protect
Secret Obsession
Love Thy Enemy
Dangerous Protector
Lethal Game
Secret Enemy
Saving Danger
Guarding Her
Deadly Protector
Danger Rising
Protecting Rebel

Redemption Harbor® Series

Resurrection
Savage Rising
Dangerous Witness
Innocent Target
Hunting Danger
Covert Games
Chasing Vengeance

Redemption Harbor® Security

Fighting for Hailey

Fighting for Reese

Fighting for Adalyn

Sin City Series (the Serafina)

First Surrender

Sensual Surrender

Sweetest Surrender

Dangerous Surrender

Deadly Surrender

Verona Bay Series

Dark Memento

Deadly Past

Silent Protector

Linked books

Retribution

Tempting Danger

Non-series Romantic Suspense

Running From the Past

Dangerous Secrets

Killer Secrets

Deadly Obsession

Danger in Paradise

His Secret Past

Paranormal Romance

Destined Mate

Protector's Mate

A Jaguar's Kiss

Tempting the Jaguar

Enemy Mine

Heart of the Jaguar